Cupid's Sweet Conspiracy

A Short Romance

The Holiday Matchmaker
Book 3

C.K. Darling

Sassy Press

Cupid's Sweet Conspiracy

XOXO
CK Darling

The Holiday Matchmaker Short Romance Series;
Cupid's Sweet Conspiracy, Book 3

First Published: January 30, 2026
Publisher: Sassy Press
Cover Designer: Booklytical Designs

Contents

Dedication

To anyone who's ever bid their heart (and their savings) on love at first sight... and to the readers who know the best investments pay off in happily-ever-afters (charitable donations optional, grand gestures required).

Chapter 1

Cupid's Sneaky Banana Bread

Nate

The whir of power tools and the steady rhythm of hammering fill the crisp February air as I survey the Hendersons' kitchen renovation. Everything's running on schedule—cabinets installed yesterday, countertops going in this afternoon. It's the smooth operation that makes me proud of what we've built at Hearthstone Homes.

"Courtney, can you confirm the timeline for the tile delivery?" I call across the work site, pulling out my project tablet to review today's schedule. As VP of client projects, coordinating these moving parts is my responsibility, but having Courtney as a project coordinator makes everything run seamlessly.

Her voice cuts through the construction noise, smooth and professional. "Delivery confirmed for two p.m. Installation crew scheduled for tomorrow morning.

I've also let the Hendersons know about the slight delay on the custom cabinet pulls—they'll be here Friday instead of Wednesday."

I should focus on the measurements I'm checking, instead, I find myself watching her through the doorway. She's got her blonde hair pulled back in a practical clip, safety glasses perched on top of her head, and she's wearing those steel-toed boots that somehow manage to look stylish on her. The woman could make a hard hat look like high fashion.

Mrs. Henderson is gesturing wildly at the breakfast nook, clearly worked up about something, but Courtney nods and pulls out her tablet. Within minutes, she's showing them a revised layout, explaining material options, and turning what looked like a potential disaster into a collaborative problem-solving session.

"And if we shift the peninsula six inches this way," she's saying, tracing the design with her finger, "we can accommodate the larger island you wanted without compromising the traffic flow."

Damn. After a year of working together, she still impresses me daily. Not only with her professional competence—though watching her handle logistics that would make seasoned contractors sweat is attractive—but with the way she genuinely cares about making our clients' dream homes come to life.

"Nate!" My name snaps me back to reality. "Dear, do you have a minute?"

I turn to find Mrs. Havers standing in the doorway, looking like she stepped out of a *Southern Living* magazine despite the construction zone around her. Her silver hair is perfectly styled, her pale pink sweater is spotless, and she's carrying a large tote bag that probably contains something that'll ruin my diet.

"Mrs. Havers. What brings you to our humble worksite today?" I set down my measuring tape and clipboard, noting how her eyes immediately dart toward where Courtney is still talking with the Hendersons.

"Oh, I was just dropping off some of my famous banana bread for the crew." She lifts an aluminum rectangle out of the tote with a smile that's maybe a little too innocent. Ever since her nephew, Wade Havers, joined the crew, she has brought baked goods by frequently, but no one is complaining. "But since I have you here, I wanted to discuss a wonderful opportunity for community involvement."

Here we go. Mrs. Havers and her "opportunities" are legendary in Peachwood Grove. Last year, her Christmas Hearts Festival resulted in my brother Brett and his wife Beth getting back together, plus she connected Dalton Grant and Savvy Whitmore, who are married now. The year before that, her holiday festival committee orchestrated three engagements, two marriages, and one very awkward but ultimately successful first date between the librarian and the bank manager.

"What kind of opportunity?" I ask warily.

"The annual Valentine's charity auction, of course! We have two exciting components this year." Her eyes sparkle with the type of mischief that should come with a warning label. "Our traditional bachelor auction where eligible men are bid on for dates, and separate silent auction for romantic experience packages donated by local businesses. It's all for such a good cause—the funds go directly to the children's literacy program."

I glance over at Courtney, who's now laughing at something Mr. Henderson said, and my stomach does this stupid flip thing it's been doing around her for months. "Sounds great, but I'm not really the bachelor auction type."

"Oh, nonsense! You're one of our most eligible bachelors in town, Nate Brockington. Successful businessman, handsome, charming—"

"Mrs. Havers, that really isn't my—"

"And it would be wonderful publicity for Hearthstone Homes. I did speak with your brother Brett. He thought it was a good idea for community relations." She's really hitting her stride now. "Plus, I was hoping Hearthstone Homes might donate money to one of the romantic experience packages for the silent auction. Perhaps a romantic getaway and activity package?"

The sound of footsteps on subflooring announces someone's approach, and I look up to find my buddy Blake McCallister ducking through the plastic sheeting. His firefighter uniform is spotless—he must be between calls—and he's wearing that smirk that usually means he's about to give me grief about something.

"Blake. What're you doing here?"

"Hendersons called about their smoke detectors. Wanted to make sure the new wiring meets code after their fire last month." He nods politely to Mrs. Havers, then his gaze shifts to where Courtney is working with our clients. He smirks because I've been talking about her non-stop for the past several months.

"Oh, wonderful! Another eligible bachelor!" Mrs. Havers clasps her hands together like she's discovered buried treasure. "I was telling Nate about our Valentine's charity auctions—both the bachelor auction and the romantic experience packages. It would be marvelous community relations for both your businesses."

Blake's smirk widens. "Nate's doing a bachelor auction? This I've gotta see."

"I didn't say I was doing it."

"Why not? Scared no one would bid on you?" And there it is. Blake's been using that tone with me since we were seventeen. He knows exactly which buttons to push.

"Scared? Right, that must be it," I say automatically.

"It's for charity, right?" Blake looks between Mrs. Havers and me like he's enjoying this way too much.

My jaw clenches. "Are you volunteering too?"

"Can't. I'm actively dating." His smile is wide and mocking. "Although, Mrs. Havers, you should hit up my brother Ryan. Being the new captain, he should bring in some heavy hitters for the cause."

"Wonderful!" Mrs. Havers beams like we've made her entire year. "Nate, I'll put you down for the bachelor auction, and Hearthstone Homes to donate a romantic experience package?"

The idea of some random women bidding on me makes my chest tight. But the thought of working with Courtney on this...

"Whatever you think is best, I'll chat it over with Brett for the donation," I reply, already second-guessing this decision. Brett will most likely laugh and hand over a check. Surely he didn't put me up for this.

"Leave everything to me." She practically radiates satisfaction. "This is going to be such a special event. I have such a good feeling about it."

Blake claps me on the shoulder. "Look at that. Brockington grows a pair."

"Shut up, McCallister."

"I should go check those smoke detectors," he says, still grinning. "But hey, I'm proud of you, man."

As he disappears into the other room, Mrs. Havers gives me a look that's uncomfortably knowing. "You know, Nate, sometimes the things we're most afraid of are exactly what we need to embrace."

"It's just a charity auction, Mrs. Havers."

"Of course it is, dear. Of course it is." Her smile is sweetness and mischief rolled into one. "I'll be in touch about the planning meetings. Enjoy that banana bread."

She glides away, leaving me standing there with the sinking feeling that I've been expertly maneuvered into something far more complicated than a simple fundraiser.

"Everything okay?"

I turn to find Courtney approaching, having apparently wrapped up the crisis with the Hendersons. Being this close to her, seeing the genuine concern in her blue eyes, reminds me why this whole auction idea has me twisted up.

"Yeah, Mrs. Havers is recruiting volunteers for the Valentine's charity auctions."

"Oh, the fundraiser! I'm helping her. It's two separate events this year—a bachelor auction and romantic experience packages silent bidding." Her face lights up with genuine enthusiasm. "Are you participating?"

"Apparently, in more ways than one. She talked me into the bachelor auction. And Hearthstone Homes is donating an experience package." I rub the back of my neck, suddenly awkward about the whole thing.

She laughs, and the sound goes straight through me. "That sounds about right for Mrs. Havers's persuasion skills."

"Are you helping to coordinate the charity event?"

"Mrs. Havers asked me to help with logistics. Making sure all the donated packages are properly cataloged, coordinating with the bachelors. She has Nic Grant handling venue details." She tucks a loose strand of hair behind her ear. "I love Valentine's Day. It's actually pretty exciting."

"It's like Valentine's Day is a commercial racket." Courtney's face falls a bit at my comment, so I quickly add, "Shouldn't dating, or being with someone, be exciting every day?"

"Ha. Nice save, and yes, I couldn't agree more." She responds with a big smile.

"Smart of her to get you involved. You're the best project coordinator I've worked with."

The compliment makes her cheeks flush slightly. "Thank you. That means a lot, especially coming from..." She trails off, seeming to catch herself.

"From your boss?" I finish, and there's something in the air between us that makes this more than workplace banter.

"Nate!" One of the crew members calls from the next room. "We need you to check these measurements before we start the backsplash."

"Duty calls," I say to Courtney, reluctant to end this conversation.

"Of course. I should get going back to the office, anyway." She walks away, then turns back. "Oh, and Nate? I think it's really generous that you're participating. The literacy program means a lot to the community."

I watch her walk away, admiring the confident way she moves, how she commands respect on a job site full of contractors, how she can switch from soothing difficult clients to coordinating complex logistics without missing a beat.

Maybe Blake was right to push me. The question is whether I'll find a way to sabotage myself before this auction ever happens.

Given my track record with women like Courtney Hartwell, I'd say the odds are about fifty-fifty.

Chapter 2

Fresh Starts and New Chapters

Courtney

"I swear this box gets heavier every time I move it," I mutter, wrestling with what feels like a container full of bricks but is actually my collection of romance novels.

"Need a hand?"

I look up to find a woman with long, light brown hair and kind brown eyes approaching from the townhouse two doors down. She's wearing leggings, tennis shoes, and a fleece jacket.

"I'm Lia Reed," she says, reaching for one end of the box without waiting for my answer. "Dr. Lia Reed technically, but nobody calls me that unless they're bleeding."

"Courtney Hartwell. And yes, please, before I throw out my back." Together we managed to get the box into my living room. "Thank you so much. You're my neighbor?"

"Two doors down, unit 47. Emergency medicine keeps me on weird hours, so I wasn't sure when you'd be around." She glances around my partially unpacked living room. "ER doctor. Yesterday was a twelve-hour shift that felt like twenty-four, but today's my day off."

"That must be intense work."

"Some days more than others." Lia settles onto my couch without invitation, which seems natural rather than presumptuous. She nods toward the romance novel box. "Speaking of normal human things, that's quite a collection."

Heat floods my cheeks. "I might have a slight addiction to happily-ever-afters."

"There's nothing wrong with that. We all need our escapes." Lia gets comfortable. "So, what brings you to Peachwood Grove? Work?"

"Work, and a fresh start." I sink into the chair across from her. "I'm a project coordinator at Hearthstone Homes. Been there a year now."

"The construction company? I know them. Good reputation."

"That's the one. Do you know the owner, Brett Brockington?"

"Not well, but his wife Beth comes into the ER occasionally with their twins. Typical boy injuries—scrapes, suspected broken bones that turn out to be sprains." Lia grins. "Those kids are adorable chaos."

I laugh, thinking of the few times I've been around Brodie and Benjamin. "That sounds about right."

The move to Peachwood Grove had been about starting over after Marcus. About finding a place where people would get to know me for who I was, not make assumptions based on my family's money or where I went to school. Here, I was Courtney, the project coordinator, not "the trust fund girl" Marcus had once introduced me as, until I set him straight.

"So, what's the fresh start about? Bad breakup?" Lia asks with the directness that probably makes her good at her job.

"Baseball player in Atlanta, Marcus Manning. Thought we were ready for the major leagues, but apparently I was more like spring training." I start placing books on my shelf. "What about you? What brought you to Peachwood Grove?"

"Burnout, mostly. I was working trauma in Atlanta, hundred-hour weeks, sleeping in on-call rooms more than my own bed. Small-town ER is still demanding, but at least here I can remember why I became a doctor." She shrugs. "Plus, I negotiated a deal that pays off my medical school loans for a five-year commitment."

"Any regrets?"

"Not really. Though I do miss having more than three restaurants that deliver, but the town keeps growing, or so I'm consistently told." Lia picks up the book I'm reading for Mrs. Havers's romance book club. "You settling in okay? Meet any interesting neighbors yet?"

"So far, only you." I pause, thinking about the last several months at Hearthstone Homes, and Nate, who's been occupying way too much of my mental real estate. "Though there is this guy at work..."

"Ah, now we're getting to the good stuff." Lia leans forward with interest. "Spill."

"Nate Brockington. He's Brett's younger brother and the VP of client projects and crews, so technically my boss." I can sense my cheeks warming. "He's... kind, strong, amazing hands, handsome. Dark hair, incredible brown eyes, and he's got this quiet confidence that's..."

"And?"

"And nothing. He's my boss." I fidget with a throw pillow. "Besides, I don't even know if he's interested. I could be reading too much into friendly workplace interactions."

"Have you tried asking him out?"

I nearly choke. "What? No! We work together, Lia. One wrong move and I could be out of a job worst case, or just die of embarrassment every day I work with him."

"Or not." Lia's expression is patient but pointed. "Look, I'm not saying be careless, but life's short. If there's chemistry, maybe it's worth exploring."

Before I can respond, there's a knock at my front door. "Expecting someone?" Lia asks.

Mrs. Havers stands on my doorstep with a covered dish and a smile that could power the entire town.

"Courtney, dear! I hope I'm not interrupting anything important."

"Not at all, Mrs. Havers. Please come in." I step

aside, noting how her eyes immediately assess my partially unpacked living room.

"Hello, Dr. Reed! Good to see you outside of the hospital." Mrs. Havers sets her dish on my coffee table. "How are you settling into our little community?"

"Very well, thank you. Everyone's been incredibly welcoming." Lia stands to shake hands.

"Excellent. Community is so important, and small towns are the best, don't you think?" Mrs. Havers turns back to me. "I brought you some chicken and dumplings. I remember how exhausting moving can be."

"That's so thoughtful, thank you." The smell is absolutely divine. I really love how Mrs. Havers looks out for everyone, but lately, having her around me is like a sense of family, and it isn't as lonely.

"Actually, I wanted to discuss the Valentine's charity auction with you, dear." Mrs. Havers settles onto my loveseat like she's planning to stay awhile.

"Of course! I'm excited to help coordinate."

"Wonderful. Now, I've had some very interesting developments today." Mrs. Havers's eyes practically sparkle with mischief. "We've got several new bachelors, including some you might find particularly... interesting."

Something in her tone makes my stomach tighten. "Oh?"

"Nate Brockington, for one. I spoke with him this afternoon, and he's agreed to participate in the bachelor auction. Plus, Hearthstone Homes is donating a romantic experience package for the separate prize auction."

My mouth goes dry at Nate's name. He already told me about it, but now it hits that some woman is going to win him, and I'm going to have to coordinate the whole thing while pretending I don't care.

"That's... that's great for the charity," I manage.

"Isn't it?" Mrs. Havers is watching my reaction closely. "Now, as the coordinator, you'll need to work very closely with all our bachelor participants to make sure they understand the process, help them plan their date offering, that sort of thing. Are you still okay with that arrangement?"

Working closely with Nate, no less, on dating packages. While I try to pretend I don't want him to take me out on a date, or kiss me, or—this is either going to be the best thing that's ever happened to me or absolute torture. "Of course. I'm so excited to help out." I respond.

"Excellent. I'll email you the full list of participants tomorrow." Mrs. Havers stands to leave, then pauses. "Oh, and Courtney? Don't forget romance book club next week—bring Dr. Reed. I recall Sophia isn't able to make it, so we have an opening."

I walk her to the door and give her a big hug. "Thank you again for the chicken and dumplings. One day you need to show me how you make them!"

"Of course, come by anytime. Also, I have a good

feeling that something wonderful is right around the corner for you, sweetheart."

After she leaves, Lia and I sit in silence for a moment.

"Okay," Lia says finally. "That woman is terrifying."

"She's not terrifying; she's connected. She's like the unofficial savant of Peachwood Grove. Knows everyone, organizes everything, and somehow always manages to be exactly where she needs to be."

"And did you catch how she was watching your face when she mentioned Nate?"

Heat floods my cheeks again. "What do you mean?"

"Come on, Courtney. I just met you, but I'm not blind. She knows you have a thing for this guy, and she's orchestrating opportunities for you to spend time with him." Lia grins. "I like her already."

"It's not that simple. We work together, and now I'm coordinating an event where he's literally being auctioned off to other women. How is that supposed to help anything?"

"Well, you could always bid on him yourself."

"I'm coordinating, I shouldn't."

"Why not?"

"Because it's..." I struggle to find the right words. "Because what if he's horrified by the idea? What if—"

"What if he's thrilled?" Lia interrupts. "What if he's been hoping for an excuse to ask you out but hasn't because he is your boss and the whole don't-crap-where-you-eat thing is in his head?"

When she puts it like that, my concerns seem less rational. The thought of someone else winning a date with Nate sends a spike of jealousy through me that I have no right to feel. But maybe—just maybe—this auction could be exactly the opportunity I've been afraid to create for myself.

Chapter 3

Peach Scones and Dating Plans

Nate

The bell above the door of Sweetheart Scones & Stories chimes as I enter, and I'm immediately hit with the scent of sweet baked goods and coffee.

Mrs. Havers has claimed the large corner table for our auction planning meeting and has already arranged it with folders and clipboards.

"Nate! Right on time," she calls out, waving me over. "I've got tea and fresh peach scones coming. Callie created a special tea blend called Holiday Matchmaker, inspired by me—can you believe that!"

"That's amazing, but you didn't have to go to all this trouble, Mrs. Havers."

"Nonsense. Good planning requires proper fuel. And what kind of proper Southern lady would I be without the offerings of food." She gestures to the chair across from her. "Courtney should be here any minute."

As if summoned, the door chimes again and

Courtney steps inside, looking slightly frazzled. She's ditched her typical professional attire for snug dark jeans and a plush powder-blue sweater that somehow transforms her eyes into mesmerizing pools of sapphire, making them even more captivating than they normally are when she's directing construction crews and managing client meetings.

"Sorry I'm late," she says, unwinding a white scarf. "I got caught up on a call with the Morrison project suppliers."

In the year we've worked together, I've learned to read Courtney's moods from these small details. The way she handled that supplier call—probably prevented a delay that could have cost us thousands.

"No worries at all, dear." Mrs. Havers beams as Courtney settles into the chair next to me—close enough that I catch a hint of her vanilla and floral perfume.

"So," Mrs. Havers says, opening the first folder, "let's talk about our auction components. Nate, you're participating in the bachelor auction, and Hearthstone Homes is donating a romantic experience package for the separate prize auction. Correct?"

"Yes, ma'am. That's what we agreed to, although for the romantic experience, Brett and I have a check cut, and you can manage what package it would fit. Does that work?"

"Wonderful!" she responds as I hand her the envelope. "Courtney will be working with each bachelor to develop their date offerings for the bachelor auction, so I'll let you focus on that today."

Courtney pulls out her tablet. "I've created templates for the bachelor auction. We need to discern what kind of date you're offering—dinner, activities, that sort of thing. For the company's donated package, we have some options that the donated funds can support."

She slides the tablet across the table to me, and our fingers brush when I reach for it. The contact is warm, and I relish how delicate her fingers and hands are. Her nails are always short and a pale color if she wears polish at all. Courtney tends to be all-natural and classic rather than hiding behind thick makeup or bright colors.

"For the bachelor auction," she continues, her voice professional despite the slight flush in her cheeks, "we'll need preferred restaurants, activities, any restrictions, transportation arrangements."

"I hadn't really thought about the details." This is more complicated than I expected.

"That's what I'm here for." She clicks her pen and looks up at me expectantly. "Let's start with the type of date. What kind of atmosphere are you thinking of? Casual and fun, or more elegant and romantic?"

The way she says "romantic" makes my mouth go dry. The idea of planning a romantic evening with some stranger while the woman I'm interested in, is coordinating the date is confusing.

"I... what do you think works best for these kinds of things? Does the date impact bidding range?"

Mrs. Havers responds. "No, not typically, it's all about the bachelor in my experience. The actual venue is secondary, typically."

"The auction date depends on what you're comfortable with and what kind of experience you want to create." Courtney tilts her head, studying me. "Are you hoping to make this feel like a real date, or more like a friendly evening out?"

Mrs. Havers is watching this exchange with barely concealed delight. "Why don't you two discuss the options while I check on those scones?"

She bustles away, leaving Courtney and me alone, feeling the unexpected pressure of arranging an intimate outing.

"Honestly?" I say, running my hand through my hair. "I have no idea what I'm doing here."

"The auction?"

"The whole thing feels weird—planning a date for someone I've never met. Standing up on a podium while people bid on me based on this date, me, and of course, the charity."

Courtney's expression softens, and I catch myself making assumptions about what she'd want in a date—in me. Someone with her background, her education—she probably expects five-star restaurants and expensive entertainment.

"It doesn't have to be complicated, Nate. What would you enjoy doing?"

The question catches me off guard. "What I'd enjoy?"

"It's your date too. You should plan something you'd actually want to do, not only what you think will impress someone." Her voice is gentle but pointed. "What makes you happy?"

The simple question undoes something in my chest. When's the last time someone asked me that?

"Honestly? I'd rather showcase what makes Peachwood Grove special than try to compete with fancy city venues." I lean forward, warming to my sudden idea. "Dinner at Magnolia Moon—their patio is nice in the evening with the string lights and outdoor heaters. Maybe a walk through downtown afterward, and see the historic district."

"That sounds perfect." Her smile is genuine, and encouraging. "Personal and authentic. Much better than some generic expensive restaurant."

"You think?" I study her face, surprised by her enthusiasm. "It's not too… simple, too boring?"

"Simple doesn't mean boring, Nate. Some of the best dates are the ones where you actually get to know each other." She makes notes on her tablet. "What about ending with coffee and dessert somewhere?"

"Willow Tree Café? They stay open late on weekends."

"Perfect. That gives a nice arc to the evening—dinner, walk, coffee. Easy to extend if things are going well, easy to wrap up if they're not."

Mrs. Havers returns with scones that smell like heaven. "How are we coming along?"

"I think we have a good plan for Nate's bachelor auction date," Courtney tells her. "Dinner at Magnolia Moon, a walk through downtown, dessert and coffee at Willow Tree Café."

"Oh, that sounds lovely!" Mrs. Havers makes notes in her folder before turning to Courtney with an expression that seems too knowing. "As our coordinator, you'll need to be prepared for any last-minute adjustments."

"Of course. I'll make sure everyone has my contact information."

"Excellent. Now, you'll both need to work together closely over the next two weeks to finalize everything. Individual meetings or phone calls to go over details, answer questions..."

Mrs. Havers launches into descriptions of other auction items, but I keep getting distracted by Courtney sitting next to me. The way she takes precise notes and her perfect handwriting. The way she asks thoughtful questions about logistics. The way she absently tucks her hair behind her ear when she's concentrating.

The irony isn't lost on me—I'm planning a romantic evening while sitting next to the woman I'd want to share it with.

"Individual meetings are for what?" The question brings me back to the conversation.

"Only to make sure everyone's comfortable and

confident," Mrs. Havers explains. "To review details and do a little coaching, if needed."

"Coaching?" I ask.

"How to present yourself, what to say during your introduction, that sort of thing." Mrs. Havers glances between us. "I think you two, would work very well together on this. Call me if you need anything else dear, I need to get home to Henry."

Mrs. Havers starts packing up with the satisfied air of someone who's accomplished exactly what she set out to do.

"What kind of coaching do you think I need? Like not showing up in my work clothes?" I chuckle. "I do own a few suits, I'll have you know. I clean up well enough."

Courtney sets down her pen and meets my gaze, clearly enjoying this. "Well, since it's Valentine's Day..." She leans forward slightly, and I catch another hint of her vanilla and floral perfume. "You'll want to embrace the romance of it all. Maybe a red tie? Something that shows you're not afraid to play up the theme?"

The way she says "embrace the romance" makes my mouth go dry. There's something different in her voice—more confident, almost flirtatious.

"You think I need help with being romantic?"

"I think," she says, her cheeks flushing pink but her gaze steady on mine, "that whoever bids on you should detect that you're taking this seriously, and that it shows you can have fun with it too."

I swallow hard, looking down at the neat event plans on the table before daring to voice my real fear.

"What if no one bids on me at all?" The words come out quieter than I intend. "I mean, we're planning this whole date, but what if I'm standing up there, and everyone just... stares? Talk about hometown humiliation."

The thought of being on that stage with dead silence makes my skin crawl. I've never been one to seek the spotlight, and the idea of being rejected is my worst nightmare.

"Are you serious?" Courtney's eyes widen, genuine surprise crossing her face. She puts her hand on my forearm, her touch light but firm. "Nate, you're going to have plenty of bidders. Trust me."

"You can't know that."

"Actually, I can." She shakes her head as if I'm being ridiculous. "You're smart, successful, and—" she pauses, a slight blush coloring her cheeks, "attractive. Half the women in town already ask about you. Mrs. Havers will probably have to implement a bidding limit to give everyone a fair chance."

The sincerity in her voice catches me completely off guard. My chest tightens, and I sense heat spreading across my face. For a moment, I can't think of anything to say—can't think of anything except how she's looking at me like she means every word.

"Well," I manage finally, clearing my throat, "as long as it's not old Ms. Gludge placing the winning bid."

"Who's Ms. Gludge?"

"My old high school principal, who is about eighty-five now."

We both laugh, and the tension from moments before transforms into something warmer, more comfortable. As we finish our scones and say our good-byes, I hold the door open for Courtney.

"I'll see you at the Henderson site tomorrow?" I ask as we reach our vehicles, though part of me wants to keep this conversation going.

"Of course." She pauses with her hand on her car door, looking back at me. "And Nate? Don't overthink the auction. Be yourself—red tie and all. That's more than enough."

I watch her drive away, her words echoing in my head. The way she looked at me when she talked about me, about being smart, successful, attractive—like she saw something in me herself worth bidding on.

For the first time since agreeing to this auction, I'm not just hoping to survive it. I'm starting to wonder if maybe the right person might place that winning bid.

Chapter 4

Sizzling Shifts and Sweet Nerves

Courtney

"Okay, spill everything. And I mean everything."

Lia kicks off her shoes and settles cross-legged on my couch, a bottle of wine in one hand and two glasses in the other. She's still in scrubs from her hospital shift, but she insisted on stopping by for "an emergency neighbor consultation" after I texted her about today's coffee meeting with Nate.

"There's nothing to spill," I say, accepting the wine she pours. "We discussed his auction date."

"Uh-huh. And that's why you've been pacing around your living room?" Lia fixes me with a direct stare that probably makes her patients confess symptoms they were trying to hide. "Come on, Courtney. What happened?"

I sink into the chair across from her, finally allowing myself to think about this afternoon. "He was—sweet and funny, and a little nervous, which was actually adorable."

"He wants to take you on that date, I bet."

"There were these moments..." I trail off, trying to put into words the way Nate looked at me when I was reassuring him and easing his nervousness. "I might have been flirting with him while we planned his date."

"And how did he respond to this alleged flirting?"

Heat floods my cheeks at the memory. "He flirted back. I think. Or maybe I was imagining it because I wanted him to." I take a larger sip of wine. "This is such a mess, Lia. I'm supposed to be coordinating this auction professionally, and instead I'm developing feelings for one of the bachelors."

"Developing feelings? Honey, you've had feelings for this man. The question is what you're going to do about it. And this charity is not your day job—you can totally bid on him. In fact, I'd bet my monthly salary that Mrs. Havers is counting on it."

I swirl the wine in my glass. "I think I want to bid on him. I mean, I'd love to go on that date that was planned. But is that crazy? We work together, and he's technically my boss."

"If working together was such a barrier, you wouldn't be sitting here looking like a lovesick teenager," Lia points out. "And workplace romance isn't nearly as complicated as dating a married man who swears he's separated."

I wince. "Still no word from Dr. Liar?"

"Nope. And that's for the best." Lia tops off our glasses. "So, tell me about these other bachelors. Anyone I should consider bidding on?"

"Well, there's Ryan McCallister. He's the fire captain." I pull out my phone and scroll through the promotional materials. "Here's his photo."

Lia leans over to look, and her eyes widen appreciatively. "Well, hello there, Captain McCallister."

"He's really nice too. His date is a cooking class up on the mountain."

"A firefighter who cooks?" Lia raises an eyebrow. "Interesting. Very interesting."

"So, you might bid?" I ask, probing her by pouring more wine in her glass.

"I might." Lia's smile turns contemplative. "God knows I deserve something good after that disaster with Chris. Finding out your boyfriend of six months has a wife and two kids…" She shakes her head.

"That totally sucks, Lia. I'm so sorry."

"Yeah, well. At least I found out before I got in any deeper." She shrugs. "Now I'm free to bid on hot bachelors at charity auctions."

We both laugh, and for a moment, I'm lighter about everything.

"You know what I hate?" I say, the wine loosening my tongue. "Everyone always assumes because I went to private school, and my family has money that I'm looking for some polished executive type. Marcus, my ex, once introduced me as 'the trust fund girl' like that was my whole identity. But it's not even my money—it's my family's. And it's not who I am."

"And Nate doesn't do that?"

"No, not at all. He asks what I think. Like my opinion matters because of my brain, not my bank account or some perceived status." I lean forward. "This morning, when we were at the job site, he asked what I would enjoy doing if I was in his place for the auction."

"That's significant," Lia says thoughtfully. "He's totally flirting with you and testing the waters. He's into you."

"You think?" I can't help the hopeful note that rises in my voice, my heart fluttering a little at the possibility. It's been so long since I've felt this kind of nervous excitement about someone, like I'm back in high school with a crush rather than a professional woman in her thirties. The wine has made me more transparent than usual, my emotions dancing clearly across my face as I lean toward Lia, desperate for confirmation that I'm not reading too much into Nate's actions.

"Absolutely. Classic interested-guy behavior." She leans forward. "But there's one more thing to consider. If you're thinking about bidding on him, you need to think about the workplace implications because that will be public right off the bat."

My stomach tightens. "What do you mean?"

"Well, finding out if he's interested and being

together in small settings is one thing. Throwing your hand up to bid in front of an audience in Peachwood Grove is another. Now, don't get me wrong, you need to go for it. I mean I would, but let me remind you, that you were the one debating it."

I drop my head into my hands. "God, why does this have to be so complicated?"

"Because nothing worthwhile is ever simple," Lia says softly. "But here's the thing—you moved here for a fresh start, right? To be somewhere people would get to see the real you?"

I nod.

"Well, maybe this is part of that fresh start. It's not like anyone would assume you got your position by sleeping to the top, you had this position well ahead of this. It's worth the risk."

"So, you might bid on Captain McCallister?"

"I might." Lia's smile turns contemplative, then rueful. "Though I should mention I made a promise to myself to swear off hotshot firefighters, and well, hotshot anythings, some time ago."

My curiosity piques. "Now that, sounds like there's a story there."

"Oh, there's definitely a story." Lia drains her wine glass and glances at the bottle. "But we're going to need a lot more wine before I dive into that particular disaster."

I laugh, already reaching for the bottle. "Well then, it's a good thing we have all evening."

"Promise me you'll give it a shot with Nate if I consider breaking my firefighter moratorium?"

I take a deep breath, experiencing a flutter of excitement that replaces some of my anxiety. "Fine. Let's put ourselves out there."

Chapter 5

Chinese Takeout and Confessions

Nate

The construction trailer at the Morrison project site is supposed to be empty by six p.m., but I spot the warm glow of the desk lamp through the windows as I pull up in my truck. Only one person would still be here this late, and judging by the frustrated sigh I can hear even from outside, Courtney's having the kind of evening that requires backup.

I grab my thermos of water and the bag of Chinese takeout I picked up on a whim—call it contractor's intuition, but when project coordinators work past sunset, they usually forget to eat.

"Knock knock," I call out as I climb the metal steps to the trailer door. "Please tell me you're not planning to sleep here tonight."

Courtney looks up from her laptop, her usually perfect hair escaping from its short ponytail and her reading glasses perched on her nose. She's surrounded by sample boards, fabric swatches, and what looks like enough paperwork to wallpaper the house we're building.

"Nate! What are you doing here?" She takes off her glasses and tries to smooth her hair, which only makes her look more adorable. "I thought you'd gone home hours ago."

"I had, but I drove by and saw the light." I hold up the takeout bag. "Figured you might need sustenance. When's the last time you ate something that wasn't from a vending machine?"

The guilty look on her face tells me everything.

"That's what I thought." I clear a space on the small table in the corner of the trailer, pushing aside rolls of blueprints and material samples. "Come on, take a break. The Morrison project isn't going anywhere, and you'll think more clearly with some actual food in you."

The Hearthstone Homes trailer is one of our nicer setups—Brett insisted on upgrading from the cramped, dingy boxes most contractors use. This one has real lighting, a small kitchenette, comfortable seating, and enough space for client meetings when on-site. Right now, though, it's intimate in a way that has nothing to do with the square footage and everything to do with the woman sitting across from me.

"You didn't have to bring me dinner," Courtney says, but she's already reaching for the container of lo mein I've set in front of her. "Though I have to admit, this smells amazing."

"Jade Garden. Best Chinese food in three counties." I settle into the chair across from her, noting how the lamplight catches the gold highlights in her blond hair. "So what's got you working until all hours? Last I checked, the Morrison project was ahead of schedule."

She takes a bite of lo mein and closes her eyes with a little sound of pleasure that makes my pants a little tight on my crotch. "It was until Mrs. Morrison decided she wants to change the master bathroom tile. Again. For the third time."

"Ouch. Let me guess—she found something new on Pinterest?"

"Instagram this time. Apparently, her sister recently redid her bathroom in Savannah, and now Mrs. Morrison wants something 'even more stunning.'" Courtney makes air quotes around the phrase, then laughs. "I've been trying to figure out how to make her vision work without going over budget or pushing back the timeline."

I lean back in my chair, studying her. Most project coordinators would have handed this problem off to someone else or told the client it was too late for changes. But Courtney's here at eight p.m. on a Wednesday, determined to find a solution that makes everyone happy.

"You know," I say carefully, "as your supervisor, I should probably point out that you don't have to solve every client crisis single-handedly."

Her expression shifts slightly at the reminder of our

professional hierarchy. "But this is my project, and I want it to be perfect." She sets down her chopsticks and rubs her temples. "Besides, I still feel like I need to prove myself sometimes."

"Courtney." I lean forward, my voice gentle but firm. "You've been here over a year, and you're the best project coordinator we've ever had. You already had the scheduling chops, and you've picked up the construction timelines, and crew management. You've more than proven yourself."

"Have I?" She looks up at me, and I sense the uncertainty in those blue eyes. "Sometimes I wonder if I'm really cut out for this, or if I'm just good at faking it until I make it."

The vulnerability in her admission surprises me. "What makes you say that?"

She takes a deep breath, seeming to gather her courage. "Can I be honest with you about something?"

"Always."

"Growing up, everything was handed to me. The best schools, the right connections, doors that opened because of my family's money." She picks at her container of rice, not meeting my eyes. "I never had to struggle for anything real. Moving here, taking this job—it's the first time I've tried to make it completely on my own."

I'm quiet for a moment, processing what she's told me. I never would have guessed that someone as competent and confident as Courtney wrestled with these kinds of doubts.

"For what it's worth," I say finally, "Brett and I hired you because you impressed the hell out of us in that interview. Not because of your family name, but because you knew your stuff, and you weren't afraid to challenge some of his ideas about project management."

"Really?"

"Really. And watching you work?" I lean forward, wanting her to notice the sincerity in my face. "You've earned every bit of respect you've gotten here. The clients love you, the crews listen to you, and you've streamlined our processes in ways that have saved us thousands of dollars."

A soft smile crosses her face. "Thank you. That means a lot, especially coming from you."

"Why from me specifically?"

"Because you don't give false praise. If you say something, you mean it." She takes another bite of lo mein, then looks at me curiously. "What about you? Do you ever feel like you don't belong?"

The question hits closer to home than I expected. "More often than I'd like to admit."

"Really? But you're so confident, respected, successful—"

"I'm also someone who spent his late teens and early twenties making every wrong choice I could find." The words come out more bitter than I intended. "After my dad died, I went off the rails hard. Partying, drugs, getting into fights. My brother Brett basically had to save me from myself."

Courtney sets down her chopsticks and gives me her full attention. "Nate—"

"You want to understand why I was so nervous about the auction? It's not just because I've never done one before. It's because sometimes I'm that screwed-up kid, wondering if anyone could look past the mistakes to find something worth keeping." I run my hand through my hair, wondering why I'm telling her this. "Some days I still can't believe I turned it around."

"But you did turn it around," she says firmly. "And not because your brother saved you, but because you chose to save yourself. You chose to get clean, to learn the business, to become the man you are now. That takes incredible strength."

"It doesn't come across like a strength. Sometimes it's like I'm still one bad decision away from screwing it all up."

"We all feel that way sometimes." Her voice is gentle, understanding. "The difference is that you've proven you can make good choices when it matters. You've built something real, something you can be proud of."

The way she's looking at me—like she really sees me, mistakes and all, and isn't running away—does something to me. Warms something inside me I didn't even realize was cold.

"How did you get so wise, Courtney Hartwell?" I ask softly.

She laughs, and the sound fills the small trailer. "Years of therapy and making my own mistakes. Plus, a slight addiction to romance novels, which has taught me that everyone deserves to be the hero of their own story."

"Romance novels?" I can't help grinning. "Should I be surprised that someone with 'Hart' in her name has a soft spot for love stories?"

"Oh god, you're not going to start making heart jokes, are you? Because I've heard them all." But she's smiling as she says it, her cheeks flushing slightly. "My college roommate thought it was hilarious that Courtney Hartwell was a hopeless romantic."

"Are you? A hopeless romantic, I mean."

"Probably more than what is good for me." She ducks her head, suddenly seeming shy. "I'm the girl who still gets excited about Valentine's Day, who believes in grand gestures and happily-ever-afters. Pretty ridiculous for someone who's supposed to be a hard-nosed project coordinator in construction, right?"

"It's perfect," I say, and I mean it. The idea of Courtney curled up with romance novels, believing in fairy tale endings, only makes her more real. "The world needs more people who believe in happy endings."

"What about you? Do you believe in them?"

"I'm starting to," I admit, looking directly into her eyes. "More than I used to, anyway."

The air between us shifts, becoming charged with something I can't quite name. Courtney's looking at me like she's seeing something new, and I realize she's looking at me like she wants me to lean closer.

Maybe I've been so busy thinking I wasn't good enough that I missed all the signs that she might want me too.

"So," I say, clearing my throat and gesturing to her laptop, "about Mrs. Morrison's tile crisis. Want to show me what she's got her heart set on? Maybe we can brainstorm a solution."

"You don't have to help with this. You've already put in a full day—"

"Courtney." I wait until she meets my eyes. "I want to help. Besides, two heads are better than one, right?"

She hesitates for a moment, then slides her laptop around to show me the screen. "Okay, so here's what she originally chose..."

As she walks me through the options, I find myself watching her more than the screen. The way she gestures when she talks, the little crease between her eyebrows when she's concentrating, the way she lights up when she finds a potential solution.

"What if we use her new tile choice as an accent?" I suggest, leaning closer to point at the screen. "Keep the original tile for the main areas—both tiles coordinate well together. We use the new one for the shower surround and maybe a border?"

"That could work," she says, her voice slightly

breathless. I realize I'm close enough to catch the scent of her perfume, close enough to spy the flecks of gold in her blue eyes. "We'd need to recalculate the quantities, but it shouldn't impact the timeline too much."

"It gives Mrs. Morrison her Instagram-worthy bathroom without blowing the budget."

"Nate, you're brilliant." She turns to face me fully, and suddenly we're inches apart. "I can't believe I didn't think of that."

"That's why we make a good team," I say softly.

For a moment, neither of us moves. The trailer seems smaller, more intimate, and I can hear her breathing. I could kiss her right now. Should kiss her. Want to kiss her more than I've wanted anything in a long time.

Just as I start to lean in, my phone rings, shattering the moment.

Brett's name flashes on the screen, and I curse under my breath. "I should probably take this."

"Of course," Courtney says, sitting back in her chair, but I can sense the disappointment in her eyes.

"Hey, Brett, what's up?"

"Sorry to bother you so late, but I need the Henderson contract details for the insurance paperwork. Can you pull from your computer?"

I glance at Courtney, who's busying herself with packing up her laptop. "I'm at the Morrison site. What specifically do you need?"

The conversation takes five minutes, but by the time I hang up, the intimate atmosphere has evaporated.

Courtney's back in professional mode, gathering her things and avoiding my eyes.

"I should probably head home," she says finally. "It's getting late, and I have that early meeting with the kitchen cabinet supplier tomorrow."

"Right. Of course." I help her gather her things, trying to recapture the easy intimacy we'd shared before the phone call interrupted us. But the moment is gone.

"Thank you for dinner and the brainstorming session. You probably saved me hours of frustration." She slings her bag over her shoulder and looks up at me. "Nate? What you said earlier, about not feeling like you're worth something? You're wrong. Just so you know."

"Courtney—"

"I'm serious. You're one of the good ones, Nate Brockington. Don't let anyone, including yourself, convince you otherwise."

As I watch her walk to her car, I'm struck by how much has changed between us in the span of an hour. We crossed some invisible line tonight, shared things we'd never told each other before. And for the first time since I started wanting Courtney, I'm not concerned by it being complicated.

I'm excited by it.

Chapter 6

Romance and Red Ties

Courtney

The next evening, Lia and I step out of Sweetheart Scones & Stories, our arms full of books and pastries, and our hearts full of romantic possibilities. Mrs. Havers's romance book club always leaves me dreamy and optimistic, but tonight there's an extra flutter of excitement in my chest.

"I can't believe you've never read a Brittany Quinn novel," I tell Lia as we walk toward our cars. "The way she writes banter between her characters is absolutely perfect."

"I'm more of a dark romance girl," Lia admits, juggling her book bag and purse. "Give me a bad boy who's secretly a saint as a sexy fae or vampire any day."

"That's very specific."

She laughs. "What can I say? I have a type—the nonexistent type."

We pause between our cars, neither quite ready to

end the evening. The downtown square is beautifully lit, the workers at the community center across the street are putting finishing touches on decorations for the Valentine's charity event.

"I still can't believe Valentine's Day is only two days away," I say, watching the twinkling lights being strung around the building's entrance. "And the auction is in two days."

"Are you nervous?" Lia asks, studying my face in the soft glow of the street lamps.

"Terrified," I admit. "But also excited? I keep thinking about everything we discussed in book club tonight—about heroines who are brave enough to go after what they want instead of waiting for it to come to them."

"And what do you want, Courtney?"

The question hangs in the air between us, we're not really talking about romance novels anymore. "I want to be brave. I want to stop analyzing every interaction with Nate and wondering if I'm reading too much into things. I want to take a chance."

"Even though he's your boss?"

"Especially because he's my boss." The words surprise me with their conviction. "I've spent my whole life playing it safe, doing what's expected, following the rules. Maybe it's time I broke a few."

Lia grins. "I like this version of you. Bold Courtney is much more interesting than Careful Courtney."

"Bold Courtney is new. I'm still figuring out how she works."

"Well, if you decide to bid on Nate, bold Courtney is definitely going to make an appearance."

As I drive home, I think about the conversation and the romance novels tucked in my passenger seat. Tonight's book club discussion was on second-chance romances, but what struck me most was Mrs. Havers's comment about heroines who create their own happy endings instead of waiting for them to happen.

Back at my townhouse, I spread my auction bidding materials across my coffee table—the paddles with numbers, the program Mrs. Havers provided with all the bachelor profiles, and the small amount of cash I'd planned to bring for the experience packages.

But as I look at Nate's photo in the program, my heart starts racing. He looks so handsome in his professional headshot, but it's nothing compared to seeing him in person—the way his eyes crinkle when he laughs, how his voice gets rough when he's concentrating, the gentle way he handles his nephews, and how committed he is to his brother Brett and his family.

I pick up my phone and scroll to my banking app. My savings account shows a healthy balance—money I've been setting aside for a vacation I haven't planned, furniture I haven't bought, a future I haven't quite figured out yet.

What if instead of saving for someday, I spent some of it on right now?

Before I can talk myself out of it, I transfer the money to my checking account and make a note on my phone:

Maximum bid: $1000.
For charity. For courage. For Nate.

The next evening, I stand in front of my bedroom mirror, adjusting the neckline of my black cocktail dress for the tenth time. It's my favorite dress—the one that makes me confident and sophisticated—tonight it's like armor. Beautiful, feminine, a tool for being noticed and making a move to win a date with Nate.

"You can do this," I tell my reflection. "You're smart, successful, and perfectly capable of bidding on a man at a charity auction."

My phone buzzes with a text from Lia:

On my way to pick you up. Are you ready to be scandalous?

As ready as I'll ever be. Thank you for being my backup courage.

Lia: Always. Now finish getting beautiful and let's go claim your man.

I apply one final coat of lipstick—a bold red that matches my newly discovered brave streak—and grab my clutch. Inside are my checkbook and a small compact for touch-ups. Everything I need for a night that could change everything.

The drive to the community center is both endless and far too short. Lia keeps up a steady stream of encouraging chatter, but I'm only half listening. My mind is spinning with possibilities and fears in equal measure.

What if I bid and don't win? What if I bid and do win? What if Nate doesn't want me to bid? What if he does?

"Breathe," Lia says as we pull into the parking lot. "You look gorgeous, you have a plan, and you're doing this for all the right reasons."

"What if I'm making a huge mistake?"

"Then you'll be making a gorgeous, well-dressed mistake that supports childhood literacy." She turns off the engine and faces me fully. "Courtney, I've watched you for two weeks now, talking about this man, lighting up whenever his name comes up, analyzing every conversation you two have. You're already emotionally invested. Now you're doing something about it."

I take a deep breath, checking my reflection one more time in the visor mirror. The woman staring back at me is polished, confident, and ready for whatever comes next. At least, she looks ready.

"Okay," I say, gathering my courage along with my purse. "Let's go bid on some bachelors."

The community center has been transformed into something out of a fairy tale. Soft lighting cascades from twinkling chandeliers overhead, while delicate rose and gold decorations adorn every surface, transforming the usually mundane space into something magical. The buzz of excited conversation fills the air, creating an atmosphere that's both intoxicatingly romantic and charged with electric anticipation—energy is prickling along my skin as we step through the doorway. I spot several of my Hearthstone Homes colleagues, including Brett and Beth Brockington, who wave from their table near the front.

And then I find him.

Nate.

He's standing with a group of the other bachelors near the side of the stage, and my breath catches in my throat. He's wearing a perfectly tailored dark suit that emphasizes his broad shoulders and tall frame, and—my heart skips—a pink shirt with a deep red tie and pocket square that makes him look sophisticated and romantic.

He followed my suggestion of embracing the Valentine's theme, and somehow that small detail makes this all the more real, more like he was thinking about me when he got dressed tonight.

"Well, well," Lia purrs beside me. "Your boyfriend cleans up nice."

"He's not my boyfriend," I whisper back, though I can't tear my eyes away from him.

"Yet." Lia vocalizes the exact thought that's echoing in my mind.

As if he can sense my gaze, Nate looks up and scans the crowd until his eyes find mine. The smile that spreads across his face is warm and genuine, and he raises his hand in a small wave that makes my stomach flutter.

"Did you see that?" Lia asks. "The way he lit up when he saw you? That man is hoping you bid on him."

"You think?"

"Trust me, I'm a doctor. I'm trained to read body language and vital signs. His pupils dilated, his posture straightened, and I'm pretty sure his pulse just spiked." She nudges my shoulder.

Nate is talking with his friend Blake and the other bachelors, noting how he keeps glancing in my direction. There's something in his expression—hope, maybe, or anticipation—that gives me the courage I've been looking for.

"I'm going to walk up to that podium when his name is called, and I'm going to bid on a date with the man I'm developing feelings for."

"There she is," Lia says with satisfaction. "There's Bold Courtney."

As Mrs. Havers takes the stage to begin the evening's festivities, I clutch my bidding paddle while my heart races with anticipation. Tomorrow is Valentine's Day—the most romantic day of the year—and tonight might be the night I finally stop dreaming about Nate and make it a reality.

The auction is about to begin, and for the first time in my life, I'm ready to fight for what I want.

Chapter 7

Bidding Wars and Bold Moves

Courtney

I adjust my black cocktail dress for the tenth time in five minutes, trying to calm my nerves. The Versace piece with its plunging V-neckline leaves me more exposed than I'd typically allow, the fabric is cool against my skin as my fingers trace the edge where it dips between my breasts. After what happened in the trailer last night—that almost-kiss, those intimate confessions—my heart races whenever I think of Nate's face only inches from mine, his breath warm against my lips before we pulled away.

"You look beautiful," Lia says, appearing beside me with two glasses of champagne. "Stop fidgeting. You're going to wrinkle your dress."

"I can't help it. I'm nervous." I accept the champagne gratefully. "Something about tonight feels... significant."

"Maybe because it is?" Lia is stunning in a deep blue dress that hugs her curves and highlights her warm skin tone. "And maybe because you're going to bid on him, and it'll cinch the deal, and he'll realize that you've caught the Nate bug?"

My stomach flutters at the reminder. "Am I brave enough to make that kind of statement so publicly?"

"Courtney." Lia fixes me with a direct stare. "After what you told me about last night—the personal conversations, the almost-kiss—you have to bid on him. Focus on this as you and him, the rest of it is noise." Lia waves her hand dismissively.

Mrs. Havers is everywhere at once, checking arrangements and wearing a smile that suggests she's very pleased with how everything is unfolding.

"Ladies and gentlemen, if you all could take your seats, we're about to begin!" Mrs. Havers's Southern charm of a voice carries across the room as she takes the stage. "Welcome to our first annual Valentine's charity auction, benefiting the children's literacy program!"

The crowd settles into their seats, and I find myself looking at the back of Nate's head, wishing he'd turn around one more time.

"We have two exciting components tonight," Mrs. Havers announces. "First, our romantic experience packages, which have been gifted by our very own local company sponsors and town donors. These packages were bid on anonymously through sealed bids submitted in advance. Second, our bachelor auction, which will be live bidding only—it's much more exciting to witness the competition to win a date with our eligible bachelors!"

That gets a holler from some tables, and everyone is smiling.

I take a sip of champagne, getting my liquid courage ahead of the auction.

"Our first package is a couples' spa day at Serenity Springs Wellness Resort." Mrs. Havers holds up a beautifully designed certificate. "This package was won by... Dr. Amelia Reed!"

I turn to stare at Lia, who raises her champagne glass with a satisfied smile. "We, so deserve a spa day."

My heart melts a little at her gesture. "Lia, that's so sweet! You bid on that for us?"

"New town, new friend, new traditions," she says with a grin. "Besides, after the week I've had in the ER and that whole Dr. Liar fiasco, I need some serious pampering."

Mrs. Havers continues announcing packages—dance lessons, wine tastings, couples' cooking classes—and I find myself genuinely enjoying the surprises and reactions.

"And now," Mrs. Havers says, her eyes twinkling as she picks up a familiar-looking certificate, "we have our romantic mountain getaway package. A weekend for two at Blue Ridge Mountain Resort, complete with couples' hiking, stargazing, and breakfast in bed."

I lean forward, curious who will receive such an awesome package.

"This package has been gifted by an anonymous donor to… Miss Courtney Hartwell!"

My champagne glass nearly slips from my suddenly numb fingers. "What?" I whisper.

The room erupts in applause, but I barely hear it over the rushing in my ears. Someone gifted me a romantic mountain getaway. But who? I look to Nate's table, but all the bachelors have moved and are behind the stage. And I have no opportunity to think on it because Mrs. Havers is onto the next portion of the event.

"Now for our bachelor auction!" Mrs. Havers announces after the experience packages are complete. "Our first gentleman is Fire Captain Ryan McCallister…"

Ryan takes the stage looking confident in his dress uniform, and the bidding is enthusiastic. Lia joins the bid but stops at one hundred dollars. He goes for a respectable amount to a teacher from the elementary school who looks thrilled with her win. Several other bachelors follow, each generating good-natured laughter from the crowd and averaging from two hundred fifty to three hundred twenty-five dollars. The charity is well on its way to our goal of ten thousand dollars.

And then Mrs. Havers announces Nate.

"Our next and bachelor is Nate Brockington, vice president of Hearthstone Homes, and one of our community's most eligible gentlemen." Mrs. Havers gestures as Nate walks onto the stage, and my breath catches in my throat.

He looks incredible. The dark suit fits him perfectly

as if it were made for him, and that red tie I suggested makes him look sophisticated and romantic. Though he's clearly nervous, he's trying to hide it behind a confident smile. When he scans the crowd, his gaze finds mine and lingers. I can't help but smile back at him. He seems more settled.

"Nate is offering a romantic evening that includes dinner at Magnolia Moon, a walk through our historic downtown, and coffee and dessert at Willow Tree Café," Mrs. Havers continues. "Bidding starts at fifty dollars."

"Seventy-five!" calls out a woman I don't recognize.

"One hundred!" comes another voice from the back.

The bidding climbs higher, my heart racing as I realize this is actually happening. Someone is going to win a date with Nate—the date we planned together.

"Two hundred fifty!" Shelley Landers calls out from across the room, her voice carrying that predatory tone that reminds me of high school mean girls.

My blood runs cold. Shelley Landers—with her perfectly styled blonde hair, designer dress, and entitled smirk. I grew up with her type my whole life.

"Three hundred!" I join the fray. Lia nudges me with approval.

"Three fifty!" Shelley counters immediately, looking pleased with herself.

I grip my champagne glass tighter, watching Nate's face as the numbers climb. He looks increasingly uncomfortable, and when his gaze meets Shelley's across the room, I watch him swallow, this neck tense.

"Four hundred!" calls out another voice, but Shelley only laughs.

"Four fifty!" she announces confidently.

Mrs. Havers scans the room. "Do I hear five hundred?"

Silence stretches in the air. Nate looks genuinely panicked now, his eyes searching the crowd until they find mine. There's something almost pleading in his expression.

"Going once..."

I think about the conversation we had last night. About proving myself, about taking chances, about being brave enough to claim what I want.

"Going twice..."

I'm not saving him from Shelley Landers. I'm claiming him for myself.

"Six hundred dollars!" The words burst out of me with more force than I intended.

The entire room turns to stare at me, but all I can do is watch Nate's face lighting up with relief and something that looks like joy.

Mrs. Havers grins before glancing at Shelley, who promptly puts down her paddle and raises her hands in surrender. "Sold to Courtney Hartwell for six hundred dollars!" Mrs. Havers announces, practically glowing with satisfaction. "What a wonderful contribution to our literacy program!"

My hands are shaking as the applause dies down. I

bid six hundred dollars on a date with Nate. In public. In front of half the town.

The auction concludes with the remaining bachelors, and as the crowd begins to mingle, I'm still sitting in stunned silence when Nate appears beside our table and Lia walks away.

"Thank you," he says, his voice rough with emotion. "You saved me from what would have been the longest evening of my life."

I stand. "It's for a good cause," I manage, though my heart is hammering.

"Is it?" he asks, and there's something in his tone that makes me look up at him. "The cause, I mean. Is that the only reason you bid?"

Heat floods my cheeks. "Nate…"

"Because I have to tell you, watching Shelley Landers try to buy a date with me was about as appealing as a root canal." His eyes crinkle at the corners. "But watching you bid on me? That was one of the best moments I've had all year."

Before I can respond, Mrs. Havers appears with an envelope. "Courtney, dear, the details for your mountain getaway!"

I take the envelope with trembling hands, and when I open it, a small card falls out into my hand. I read the script:

For Courtney—I hope this was worth the wait. Thank you for helping me plan the perfect evening, even though you didn't realize I only wanted it for you. In case it doesn't work out that way, here's a well-earned getaway. My grand gesture. -Nate

I stare at the card, then look up at him in shock. "You bid on the mountain package for me?"

His confident smile falters slightly, replaced by nervous vulnerability. "I was hoping… well, I was hoping you'd bid on me. The mountain getaway was only a dream for an invite, but certainly something I think you'd enjoy regardless."

"You…" I'm struggling to process this. "You anonymously gifted me a romantic getaway, and then let yourself get auctioned off, hoping I might bid?"

"When you put it like that, it sounds a little complicated," he admits, running his hand through his hair. "But yeah—that's basically what happened."

Lia is grinning beside me and gives me a small nudge. "I think I'll go find the ladies' room," she says tactfully. "Take all the time you need."

Once she's gone, Nate steps closer, his voice dropping to a rough whisper that makes my toes curl. "So, what do you say, Courtney? Will you let me take you to dinner tomorrow night? The dinner you paid six hundred dollars for?"

The way he says it—confident and hopeful and a little dangerous—makes my stomach flutter wildly. "That depends," I say, trying to match his tone even though my voice is shaking. "Are you going to make it worth my six hundred dollars?"

His smile turns wicked, and he leans in. "I plan to make it worth every penny."

And then he's kissing me, right there in the community center with half the town watching. It's not a tentative first kiss or a polite public peck. It's the kind of kiss that claims and promises while making the rest of the world disappear.

When we finally break apart, I'm breathless and dizzy.

"So," I whisper against his lips, "tomorrow night?"

"Tomorrow night," he confirms. "I'll pick you up at seven."

As I watch him walk away, I realize that Mrs. Havers was right about one thing—sometimes love does find a way.

Chapter 8

Worth Every Penny

Nate

Standing on Courtney's doorstep at exactly seven p.m., I adjust my tie for the third time and try to calm the nervous energy that's been building all day. This isn't just any Valentines date—this is the date we planned together, the one she bid six hundred dollars to win, and somehow that makes it both more and less pressure all at once.

I ring the doorbell, and within moments, the door swings open to reveal Courtney looking absolutely stunning in a cream sweater dress that hugs her curves and coordinated tights and high boots that show off her legs. Her hair falls in soft waves around her shoulders. She's so beautiful.

"Wow," I breathe, completely forgetting whatever smooth opening line I'd planned. "You look incredible."

"Thank you." Her smile is radiant, and I catch a hint

of nervousness that matches my own. "You clean up pretty well yourself."

I'm wearing my charcoal gray sports jacket with a blue oxford and navy pants. "Ready for our six-hundred-dollar date?"

She laughs, grabbing a small clutch and a light jacket. "I still can't believe I did that. In front of the entire town."

"I would have been happy to take you on this date with no auction," I tell her as I help her into my truck. "Though I have to admit, watching you outbid Shelley Landers was pretty satisfying."

"She looked like she wanted to murder me," Courtney says with a grin as I start the engine.

"I was terrified she was actually going to win."

"Were you really?" She turns to face me as we drive toward downtown. "Terrified, I mean?"

I consider the question as I navigate the familiar streets. "Terrified might be the wrong word. More like... devastated at the thought of spending my evening with someone who wasn't you."

Her breath catches slightly at my honesty. "Nate..."

"Too much?" I glance over at her, worried I'm coming on too strong.

"Not too much," she says softly. "Perfect, actually."

Magnolia Moon looks exactly like I hoped it would—the outdoor patio strung with twinkling lights, space heaters providing warmth against the February evening, and enough atmosphere to make this special. The hostess leads us to a corner table with a view of the historic downtown square, and I can't help but smile at how perfectly everything is working out.

"This is beautiful," Courtney says, looking around at the romantic setting. "I can't believe we were planning this for some random woman."

"Not random," I correct, pulling out her chair for her. "Always for you. I just didn't know how to tell you that yet."

She settles into her seat, looking up at me with an expression that makes my chest tight. "You planned this whole evening thinking about me?"

"Every detail." I take my seat across from her, reaching across the table to take her hand. "When you asked what kind of atmosphere I wanted, what would make me happy—all I could think about was what would make you smile."

Her fingers thread through mine, and I feel that same jolt of electricity I've been feeling every time we touch. "You realize this means you've essentially been courting me for weeks without my knowing it?"

"Courting?" I can't help but grin at her choice of words. "That's very romance novel of you."

"I told you I was a hopeless romantic." She ducks her head slightly, but she's smiling. "And apparently I have a thing for men who plan elaborate dates."

"Men in general, or one man specifically?"

"One man specifically," she says, meeting my eyes

directly. "One very patient, thoughtful, infuriating man who's been driving me crazy for months."

"Infuriating?"

"Do you realize how hard it's been to work with you, feeling the way I do? Trying to stay professional when all I wanted was to kiss you?"

I can't resist her confession. "Well, now you know," I say, my voice low as I lean across the table, closing the space between us. My hand finds her cheek, thumb brushing against her soft skin. Her lips part slightly in anticipation, and I kiss her properly—not the hurried moment at the auction, but deliberately, savoring the taste of her, the softness of her lips against mine. When we break apart, Courtney's eyes flutter open, her pale cheeks flushed.

"I've been wanting to do that since the Morrison project," I confess.

"Now I know," she agrees, her voice soft. "And it was worth the wait."

Our server appears with menus and wine recommendations, and we settle into the easy rhythm of a real date. We order the salmon special and a bottle of local wine, and as we wait for our food, I find myself studying Courtney's face in the candlelight.

"What?" she asks, noticing my attention.

"I'm trying to reconcile the woman sitting across from me with my colleague who spent the other night solving tile crises and eating Chinese takeout in a construction trailer."

"Same person," she says with a laugh. "Just different settings."

"I like both versions," I tell her. "Professional Courtney who can handle any client crisis, and this Courtney who's looking at me like..."

"Like what?"

"Like you're happy to be here with me."

Her expression grows serious. "Nate, I don't only want to be here with you. I've wanted to be here with you for months. I've imagined this exact scenario more times than I probably should admit."

"You've imagined dating me?"

"I've imagined a lot of things," she says, and the heat in her voice makes my pulse spike. "Dating you. Kissing you. Waking up next to you. Having the right to touch you whenever I want."

My grip on my wine glass tightens. "Courtney..."

"Too much?" she asks, echoing my earlier question.

"Not nearly enough," I say honestly. "But if you keep talking like that, I'm going to have a very hard time being a gentleman for the rest of this evening."

Her smile is knowing and coy. "Who says I want you to be a gentleman?"

Thankfully, our food arrives before I can respond to that loaded comment, giving me a chance to regain my composure. The salmon is perfect, and the conversation flows as easily as the wine. We talk about everything—work stories, childhood memories, dreams for the future—and I fall even harder for the woman across from me.

"Tell me more," Courtney says after I finished telling her about the time Brett and I tried to build a treehouse and ended up with a structure that looked more like modern art.

"Worst construction disaster?"

"Yes, these stories are the best," she chuckles.

"That wasn't a construction disaster, that was a childhood engineering failure," I protest. "But fine. The worst actual construction disaster was probably the McBride's bathroom renovation three years ago."

"What happened?"

"Let's say that when Mrs. McBride said she wanted 'something bold' for her powder room, I should have asked for clarification before approving lime green tile with hot pink grout."

Courtney nearly chokes on her wine. "You didn't."

"I did. It looked like a tropical fever dream. We had to redo the entire thing." I shake my head at the memory. "That's when I learned to always, always get approval in writing for any design choices."

"I would have loved to see that," she says, laughing. "Lime green and hot pink?"

"With gold fixtures. I can't forget the gold fixtures."

We're both laughing now, and I realize this is exactly what I wanted—this easy back-and-forth, this feeling of being completely comfortable with someone who also makes my pulse race.

After dinner, we walk hand in hand through the historic downtown area. The February air is crisp but not cold, and the old-fashioned streetlamps cast everything in a warm, romantic glow. Courtney's hand is perfect in mine, and I find myself slowing our pace, not wanting this part of the evening to end.

"Tell me something I don't know about you," she says as we pause in front of the old courthouse.

"Something you don't know?" I consider the question. "I wanted to be an architect when I was a kid."

"Really? What changed your mind?"

"Reality, mostly. My grades weren't good enough for architecture school, and after Dad died and I went off the rails... well, it wasn't really an option anymore." I shrug, surprised that talking about it doesn't hurt as much as it used to. "But I like what I do now. Building things, seeing projects come together, working with my hands."

"Do you ever regret it? Not pursuing architecture?"

"Not anymore," I say honestly. "This path led me to Hearthstone Homes, which led me to you. Hard to regret that."

She stops walking and turns to face me fully. "Nate..."

"Your turn," I say, wanting to shift the focus away from my too-honest admission. "Tell me something I don't know about Courtney Hartwell."

"I wanted to be a writer when I was younger," she admits. "Romance novels, specifically. I had this fantasy of writing sweeping love stories that would make people believe in happy endings."

"What stopped you?"

"Practicality. My parents made it clear that writing wasn't a 'real' career, that I needed something stable and respectable." She focuses on our joined hands. "I got a business degree and convinced myself that project management was close enough to storytelling."

"Is it?"

"Sometimes. When everything comes together perfectly, when a project goes from concept to completion... there's a narrative arc to it." She looks up at me. "It's similar as creating something from nothing, you know?"

"You could still write," I point out. "Evenings, weekends. There's no rule that says you can only have one passion."

"Maybe," she says, but there is a spark of interest in her eyes. "Maybe I will. But for now, consuming stories is my happy place."

We continue our walk, eventually ending up at Willow Tree Café for dessert and coffee. The café has a cozy, intimate atmosphere, and we settle into a corner booth that is private despite the other customers scattered throughout the space.

"This is perfect," Courtney says, sliding into the booth beside me instead of across from me. I love the warmth our bodies create next to each other. "The whole evening has been perfect."

"Even better than you imagined when you were

bidding on me?" I ask, putting my arm around her shoulders.

"Much better." She curls into my side, fitting perfectly against me. "I was mostly panicking and trying not to let Shelley Landers get her claws into you."

"My hero," I tease, pressing a kiss to the top of her head.

"I prefer to think of it as protecting my investment."

"Your investment?"

She tilts her head up to look at me. "My heart," she says simply.

The honesty in her voice takes my breath away. "Courtney..."

"It's fast," she says. "I get we work together and it's complicated and we should probably take things slow. But I can't pretend I don't feel this, Nate. I can't pretend that sitting here with you isn't like the most natural thing in the world."

I set down my coffee cup and turn to face her fully. "I don't want you to pretend. I don't want either of us to pretend."

"What does that mean?"

"It means I'm tired of being careful around you at work. Tired of pretending I don't want to touch you when you're explaining project timelines. Tired of acting like you're only my colleague when you're so much more than that."

Her eyes widen slightly. "Nate, we—"

"I understand. We have to be smart about this, figure

out the professional side." I take her hand, threading our fingers together. "But right now, in this moment, I only want to be honest with you."

"Okay," she says softly. "Be honest with me."

"I'm very into you, Courtney. Have been for months. And tonight, sitting here with you, talking about dreams and disasters and everything in between... I don't want this date to end."

Her breath catches. "It doesn't have to end."

"Doesn't it? Monday we go back to work, back to being professional."

"How about we enjoy the moment, be present now, and figure the rest out a little later," she says, and there's something bold in her voice that I haven't heard before. "Honestly, it's not like half the town is unaware I bid on you. You kissed me at the auction, I think it's fair to say people saw us, Nate."

"Fair point. And as long as you're okay with this, I'm absolutely okay with it."

She leans closer, her voice dropping to a whisper. "I've never been more sure of anything."

The drive back to her townhouse is charged with anticipation. We hold hands across the center console, and every red light is like an eternity. When I pull into her driveway, neither of us moves to get out of the truck.

"I don't want this to end," she says, echoing my words from the café. She turns to face me, and in the dim light from her porch, the want in her eyes is clear. "Would you like to come in? For a drink? Or..."

"Or," I say, and my voice comes out rougher than intended.

We make it to her front door before the careful control I've been maintaining all evening snaps. Before she unlocks the door, I'm spinning her around, pressing her back against it, capturing her mouth with mine.

She's as eager and responds immediately, her hands fisting in my sports coat as she kisses me back with voracious desire. She tastes like coffee and chocolate and promises, and when she makes a soft moan of pleasure against my lips, I nearly lose my mind.

"Inside," she whispers against my mouth. "Before my neighbors get a show."

We tumble through the door, never breaking contact, and I kick it shut behind us. Her living room is softly lit by a single lamp, and her novels are scattered across the coffee table, but all I can focus on is the woman in my arms.

"Courtney," I murmur against her neck, breathing in the scent of her perfume. "God, I've wanted this for so long."

"How long?" she asks, her hands working at the buttons of my shirt.

"Since that third week you began working for us. You were wearing that blue dress, and you were arguing with the tile contractor about proper spacing, and all I could think about was how beautiful you were when you were being stubborn."

She laughs, the sound breathless and delighted. “That long?”

“That long.” I cup her face in my hands, studying her features in the lamplight. “You?”

“The Teller Real Estate project,” she admits. “You spent an hour helping me figure out the revised timeline when you could have told me to handle it myself. You were so patient, so kind, and I realized I was in trouble.”

“Good trouble or bad trouble?”

“The best kind of trouble,” she says, pulling me down for another kiss.

This time when we break apart, we’re both breathing hard, and I can see my desire reflected in her eyes. But I also see something else—trust, affection, and the promise of something deeper.

“I should go,” I say, though every cell in my body is protesting the idea.

“Should you?” she asks, and there’s a challenge in her voice that makes my pulse spike.

“If I stay…”

“If you stay, we’ll figure it out together. All of it—the work situation, the complications, everything.” Her hands rest on my chest. “I’m not asking for forever tonight, Nate. I’m only asking for now.”

“Courtney…” I’m wavering, torn between want and the knowledge that we should probably slow down. Shouldn’t we?

“I know what I want,” she says firmly. “Do you?”

I look into her eyes—those beautiful blue eyes that

have been driving me crazy for months—and there is certainty. No hesitation, no doubt. Just a woman who knows her own mind and isn't afraid to ask for what she wants. What a freaking turn-on.

"Yes," I say finally. "I want you, Courtney."

And then I'm kissing her again before she leads me toward her bedroom upstairs.

I KICK off my shoes by the bedroom door, trailing kisses down Courtney's throat as we stumble inside. "God, you're beautiful," I murmur, hands at her hips, pulling her against me, ensuring there is no space between us. The sweater fabric of her dress strains between us, and I can touch every curve, every shift of her body as she arches into me.

She tilts her head back, lips parting on a breath. "You say the sweetest things."

"Surprised?" I nip at her collarbone.

"No, but I like it when you say it."

Courtney turns to me and smiles, soft and sure, reaching for the hem of her dress pulling it up to her thighs. I stop her hand. "Let me."

She hesitates for half a second—before nodding.

My fingers trace down to her hips, and I squat down before I pull the sweater dress up slowly and kiss her thighs then, panties, and belly. Each movement of a couple of inches is rewarded with a kiss and a moan before I'm tossing it over her head and dropping it behind her. She stands there in her ivory lace bra and matching underwear, skin glowing in the dim light.

She's all curves in an hourglass figure. Christ, she's perfect.

"You're staring," she whispers.

"Can't help it." My voice is rough, throat tight. "You're absolutely a wet dream come to life."

I step closer, palms skimming up her bare arms, over her shoulders, down to the swell of her breasts. She shivers beneath my touch, and I swallow hard. Every inch of her is soft, warm, alive under my hands.

"Nate," she breathes, fingers curling around my wrists.

I kiss her again, slow and deep, pouring every unspoken thing into it—how long I've wanted this, how much I want to get it right. When we break apart, I rest my forehead against hers.

"Can I?" I ask, thumbs brushing the edge of her lace cups. "Can I touch you more?"

Her breath hitches. "Yes. Please."

That one word undoes me.

I peel the lace away slowly, baring her to me. Her breasts are full, pale, tipped with the softest pink. I kiss each one gently, reverently, before taking one into my mouth. She gasps, fingers threading into my hair.

"God, Nate—"

I roll my tongue over her nipple, feeling it tighten,

and she moans again, louder this time. I switch, giving the other the same attention, reveling in every shiver, every arch of her back.

Her hands slide down my chest, over my stomach, and I catch them before she can go further. “Wait.”

She blinks up at me. “What?”

“I need to make sure.” My voice is low, serious. “Are you sure? We don’t have to—”

“I’m sure,” she says, kissing me quickly. “I want this. I want *you*. But only if you’re sure too.”

“I’ve never been more sure of anything.”

Her smile is radiant. “Then don’t stop, Nate.”

She reaches for my belt, and undoes it with practiced ease, tugging my pants and boxers down until they pool on the floor. Her hand wraps around my shaft, and I hiss through my teeth.

“Courtney—”

“Hmm… You feel so good,” she murmurs, stroking me slowly.

I brace myself against the wall, hips jerking into her grip. “If you keep that up, this’ll be over before it starts.”

She grins, wicked and beautiful, and releases me.

I strip off my shirt and step out of my pants, kicking them aside. I reach into my wallet, pull out the condom I’ve carried for weeks now—in case, while hoping—and rip the package open.

“Watch me,” I say, rolling it on slowly, never breaking eye contact.

Her lips part. “You’re trying to kill me.”

"Not yet." I step back into her, pressing my body flush against hers. "But I will make you come. Again and again."

She laughs breathlessly, biting her lip. "Promises, promises."

I don't answer with words.

I lift her, and she wraps her legs around my waist automatically, arms locking behind my neck. I carry her to the bed, laying her down gently, hovering over her.

"Tell me what you like," I say, kissing her collarbone, then her shoulder, then the soft swell of her breast again.

"Everything," she whispers. "Touch me everywhere—don't stop."

I kiss my way down her stomach, over the curve of her hip, until I reach the delicate lace. I pull it aside and press my mouth to her.

She jerks, moaning as my tongue parts her, tasting her for the first time. She's sweet like honey, warm, wet, and I groan against her, savoring every sound she makes.

"Nate—oh god—"

I work her slowly, deliberately, building the pressure with long, deep strokes before flicking my tongue over her clit. She writhes beneath me, hands clutching the sheets.

"More, Nate, more," she begs.

I slip two fingers inside her, curling them, finding a raised nub and I rub over it, and she cries out, back arching off the bed. I keep up the rhythm, my tongue circling her clit in tight, steady motions.

She comes with a broken cry, body trembling under my hands and mouth. I don't stop, gently riding out the waves until she's gasping, boneless.

"Nate," she whimpers, fingers finding my hair. "I need you. I want you inside me."

I kiss my way back up her body, licking my lips, savoring her taste.

"I'm right here," I whisper, settling between her legs.

I guide myself to her entrance, pausing just at the edge.

"Look at me," I say.

She does, her eyes dark with desire, cheeks flushed.

"Tell me again. You want me inside you."

She nods. "Yes. I want you inside me."

I move into her slowly, giving her time to adjust. She's tight, warm, perfect—better than a dream.

"You feel incredible," I grit out, holding still for a second, fighting the urge to thrust like a wild man into her.

"Don't hold back," she whispers. "Take me with you, lose control, Nate. Show me how much you want me."

That's all I need.

I start to move, deep and steady, each thrust drawing a moan from her lips. She meets me with every stroke, her legs tightening around me, nails raking down my back.

"Harder," she gasps. "Please, Nate—"

I oblige, driving into her with more force, setting a relentless pace. She's so wet, so responsive—I can sense her starting to tighten around my cock.

"That's it, beautiful," I murmur against her neck. "Come for me. Let me feel it."

She does, crying out my name as her body clenches around my cock, dragging a groan from deep in my chest.

I don't last much longer.

My thrusts grow erratic, my vision blurring at the edges. I bury myself deep inside her, hips snapping forward as I come with a guttural sound, pleasure ripping up my back and through me like fire.

I collapse beside her, breathing hard, heart hammering. She turns her head to look at me, eyes soft, lips swollen from kissing.

"That," she says with a wide grin, "was worth every penny—for charity, of course."

I laugh hard and pull her against me. She rests her head on my chest, one hand splayed over my heart.

"If you give me a few minutes, I suggest we have charity round two. What do you think?" I ask, brushing hair from her face.

"Absolutely," she murmurs, closing her eyes.

I kiss her forehead, fingers tracing idle patterns on her bare skin.

I've never felt this full, this complete.

She's in my arms, warm and trusting, and for the

first time in years—maybe in my life—it's clear this is the woman for me. This is it.

Chapter 9

Professional Boundaries and Personal Breakthroughs

Courtney

I wake up slowly, aware of warmth and the scent of cedar and something distinctly Nate before my eyes even open. Sunlight streams through my bedroom windows, and I can hear birds singing outside—a perfect Saturday morning.

Nate's arm is wrapped around my waist, his face buried in my hair, and for a moment I lie there savoring the feeling of being held. We crossed a line last night, several times through the night, and I don't regret a single moment of it.

"Morning," he murmurs against my neck, his voice rough with sleep.

"Morning." I turn in his arms so I can see his face—hair mussed, eyes still sleepy, stubble shadowing his jaw. He looks younger like this, more relaxed than I've ever seen him. "Sleep well?"

"Best sleep I've had in months." He tightens his arm around me, pulling me closer. "You?"

"Mmm." I reach up to trace the line of his jaw with my fingertip. "I could get used to this."

"Good. Because I plan on making this a regular occurrence."

The promise in his voice sends heat spiraling through me, but reality is starting to creep in around the edges of our perfect bubble. "Nate, we do need to talk about work."

"Do we have to? Right now?" He presses a kiss to my forehead. "Can't we just pretend the outside world doesn't exist for a little while longer?"

"I wish we could, but we can't avoid it forever this weekend."

"Are you sure? I mean, it is only Saturday."

I sit up, pulling the sheet with me. "We have the Morrison project meeting Monday morning, and the Henderson follow-up Tuesday. We're going to have to work together, and I need to understand how we're going to handle that."

He sighs, sitting up beside me. "You're right. We do need to figure this out." He runs his hand through his already messy hair. "What are you thinking?"

"Honestly? I'm terrified," I admit. "Not about this," —I gesture between us—"but about people thinking I'm sleeping my way to better projects, or that you're playing favorites."

"That won't happen."

"Won't it? Nate, you're the VP of client projects. I report to you on most of my work. People are going to notice if our dynamic changes."

"Courtney, we can, of course, be professional."

I shake my head. "Of course we can. That's not what I mean."

He's quiet for a moment, considering this. "We could talk to Brett. Ask him to adjust the reporting structure so you report directly to him instead of me."

"Would he do that?"

"I don't see why not. He's always said he wants Hearthstone Homes to be a place where good people can build careers. That includes building personal lives." Nate takes my hand, threading our fingers together. "Besides, Brett's not stupid. He's probably been expecting this for months."

The thought makes me laugh despite my nerves. "Has it been that obvious?"

"To everyone except us, apparently."

Over the next week, we settle into a careful routine. At work, we maintain professional boundaries—no lingering touches, no intimate eye contact across conference tables, no private conversations that don't relate to projects. But after hours, we're inseparable.

Wednesday evening finds us at his place, attempting to cook dinner together. I say attempting because Nate wasn't exaggerating when he said he wasn't much of a cook.

"How do you burn water?" I ask, surveying the pot he's somehow managed to scorch.

"It's a talent," he says, looking genuinely puzzled. "I thought I was supposed to boil it for the pasta."

"You are. But you're supposed to put water in the pot first." I can't help laughing as I rescue the situation. "How have you survived this long?"

"Takeout, protein drinks, sandwiches, and frozen dinners, mostly. Some very patient women who took pity on me."

"Very patient women?" I raise an eyebrow, surprised by the little spike of jealousy that hits me.

"One or two over the years. Nothing serious." He comes up behind me, wrapping his arms around my waist as I fix the pasta water. "Nothing like this."

"What's this?"

"This is me falling completely, head-over-heels in love with a woman who's beautiful, brilliant, and apparently capable of saving me from my own cooking disasters."

My heart does a little flip at the L-word, even though we've been dancing around it for days. "You love me?"

"I love you," he says simply, like it's the most natural thing in the world. "It's fast, but—"

"I love you too," I interrupt, turning in his arms. "I love your terrible cooking and your patient explanations and the way you make me feel as if I can handle anything."

"You can handle anything," he says seriously. "You're the strongest person I know."

The pasta water starts boiling, and we break apart reluctantly to finish dinner. But the conversation continues as we cook together, and I realize this domestic intimacy might be even more powerful than physical attraction. This is what building a life together looks like—navigating each other's quirks, finding rhythms that work, creating new traditions.

Thursday brings our first real test. The Morrison project hits a snag when the contractor discovers a structural issue that's going to require significant modifications to our timeline and budget. It's exactly the type of crisis that requires both of our expertise, and we have to present options to the client together.

"Okay," I say as we drive to the Morrison house, "how do we handle this?"

"Like we always do," Nate says, though his hand finds mine across the center console. "We focus on the client's needs, present the options clearly, and solve the problem."

"And if Mr. Morrison asks about our personal relationship?"

"This isn't about us; it's about their house."

The meeting goes better than expected. Mr. Morrison is understandably frustrated about the delays, but our professional presentation of options and solutions wins him over. We work together seamlessly—I handle the timeline and budget implications while Nate explains the structural modifications. By the end of the meeting, we have a revised plan that everyone can live with.

It's only as we're walking back to the truck that I realize how natural it has always felt to work with him as a true partner.

"That went well," Nate says as we drive back to the office.

"It did. We make a good team."

"We always have," he points out. "Now we're just honest about it."

But Friday afternoon brings a bigger challenge. We're in the middle of a project review meeting when Sarah from accounting makes an observation that makes my blood run cold.

"I've noticed that Courtney's been getting assigned to more of the high-profile projects lately," she says, looking directly at Nate. "The Morrison renovation, the Henderson addition, the new Palmer custom build. Those are usually reserved for you or Brett."

The room goes quiet, and every eye turns toward me. Heat floods my cheeks as I realize what she's implying.

"Courtney has earned those assignments," Brett says, his voice carefully professional but with an edge that suggests he's not pleased with the direction of this conversation. "She is a director at this company, and her performance reviews speak for themselves."

"Of course," Sarah says quickly, but the damage is done. "I was only making an observation."

The meeting continues, but I can barely focus on the discussion. All I can think about is the speculation in my colleagues' eyes, the whispered conversations that are going to happen as soon as we leave this room.

After the meeting, I escape to the bathroom and splash cold water on my face, trying to calm down. This is exactly what I was afraid of. People are going to think I'm sleeping my way to better assignments, that Nate is playing favorites because we're involved.

"Courtney?" Brett's wife, Beth, is standing in the doorway, looking concerned. "Are you okay?"

"I'm fine," I lie, grabbing paper towels to dry my hands.

"No, you're not." She steps inside and closes the door behind her. "That was uncomfortable. Sarah was out of line."

"Was she wrong, though?" The words burst out before I can stop them. "Am I getting better assignments because Nate and I are... because we're..."

"Because you're dating?" Beth finishes gently. "Honey, you've been getting those assignments since before you and Nate got together. Everyone knows that."

"Do they? Or are they going to look back and rewrite history to fit their assumptions?"

Beth considers this seriously. "Some people might. But the people who matter—Brett, your clients—they realize how your work speaks for itself."

"I... I don't want people to think I didn't earn my position."

"Then don't let them." Beth's voice is firm but kind. "Hold your head high, do excellent work, and let your results speak for themselves. You already report to Brett, if someone has an issue, they can talk to him or HR."

That evening, Nate and I have our first real fight. Not a fight, exactly, but our first serious disagreement about how to handle the work situation.

"Okay," he says slowly, studying my face. "Was it what Sarah said?"

I tell him about the speculation I saw in people's eyes, about my conversation with Beth. "I don't like this, Nate. Wondering if people think I'm only successful because I'm sleeping with an owner and executive of the company."

"You're not 'only' anything," he says firmly. "You're the best project coordinator we've ever had, and everyone knows it. You were here a year before we got together, it's unfounded and ridiculous."

"Do they? Or do they just think I'm good at my job because I get easy assignments? It's not ridiculous how I'm feeling."

"Courtney, that's not—"

"Isn't it?" I can hear my voice rising, but I can't stop myself. "And I've been getting plum assignments at a rate that might look suspicious to outside observers."

"You've been getting them because it's your job, and our junior coordinators are not ready yet. Because you've proven you can handle complex projects and difficult clients."

"I know that, and you know that, but does everyone else?"

He's quiet for a moment, and he's thinking through the implications. "What do you want to do?"

"I want to talk to Brett. I want to take on a really challenging project. Something that will prove I can handle anything you throw at me."

"The Peterson estate custom build," he says immediately. "It's a nightmare project rolled into three. Difficult clients, tight timeline, complex design requirements."

"Perfect. I'll take it. Maybe, have a junior coordinator join me as support."

"Courtney, you don't understand. The Petersons have gone through three different contractors in the past six months. They're impossible to please."

"Then I'll be the one who finally pleases them." I take his hands, needing him to understand how important this is to me. "I need to do this, Nate. I need to prove—to myself and everyone else—that I can handle the hard stuff."

He studies my face for a long moment, then nods slowly. "Okay. We'll talk to Brett on Monday."

"Thank you."

"But Courtney? You don't have anything to prove to me. You never did."

MONDAY MORNING'S conversation with Brett goes better than expected. He listens to our concerns. When I ask about the Peterson project, Brett winces. "You sure you want that headache?"

"Absolutely. Well, the project and I suppose the headache you and Nate keep referring to."

"Effective immediately, Courtney, you're on the Peterson project," he says, making notes in a file. "Alright. But I'm assigning Jake Williams as your assistant project manager. If the Petersons drive you crazy, you'll have backup. Nate, you'll still be involved in the transfer and project oversight, but in an advisory capacity rather than supervisory. This should eliminate any concerns about conflicts of interest."

As we leave Brett's office, I'm lighter than I have been all week. The professional complications aren't completely resolved, but we have a plan for managing them.

"Better?" Nate asks as we walk back to our respective offices.

"Much better. Thank you for understanding why this was important to me."

"I'm proud of you," he says quietly, stopping outside my office door. "For standing up for yourself, for taking charge of the situation. That takes guts."

"I learned from the best," I tell him.

The Peterson project turns out to be every bit as challenging as advertised. Mrs. Peterson changes her mind about design elements daily, Mr. Peterson questions every budget line item, and their daughter, a real estate agent, has opinions about everything from paint colors to bathroom fixtures.

But somehow, I find myself thriving under the pressure. Every problem that arises, every crisis that threatens the timeline, becomes an opportunity to prove that I can handle anything. Jake turns out to be an excellent assistant, and together we navigate the Peterson family's demands with patience and creativity.

Three weeks into the project, I'm working late in my office when Nate appears in my doorway.

"Burning the midnight oil again?" he asks, leaning against the frame.

"I'm finishing up the Peterson timeline revisions. Again." I look up from my computer, noting how handsome he looks even under the harsh office lighting. "What are you still doing here?"

"Waiting for my girlfriend to finish work so I can take her to dinner."

The casual way he says "girlfriend" makes my heart flutter. We haven't really talked about labels, but hearing him claim me so naturally sounds so right.

"Your girlfriend is almost done," I tell him. "Just need to send this email to the Petersons and—"

My computer chimes with an incoming message, and I glance at the screen. It's from Mrs. Peterson, and the subject line makes me groan: "URGENT: Complete design change request."

"Let me guess," Nate says, reading my expression.

"Mrs. Peterson wants to tear everything down and start over?"

"Close. She wants to change the entire kitchen layout because she saw something on Pinterest that she likes better." I open the email and scan the details. "This would set us back three weeks and blow the budget by at least fifteen thousand dollars."

"What are you going to do?"

I consider my options, then start typing a response. "I'm going to give her exactly what she wants."

"Courtney—"

"But I'm going to show her exactly what it will cost —in time, money, and disruption to her family, by including Mr. Peterson." I continue typing, outlining the implications of her request in clear, professional terms. "And then I'm going to present three alternative solutions that give her the same look she wants without destroying our timeline or budget."

Nate watches me work, and when I finish the email and hit send, he shakes his head in amazement.

"You realize you handled that crisis in less than five minutes?"

"I had a good teacher," I tell him, standing up and gathering my things. "Plus, I'm learning that sometimes the best way to handle unreasonable requests is to give people exactly what they ask for—along with a clear picture of the consequences."

"Remind me never to make unreasonable requests of you."

"Oh, you can make all the unreasonable requests you want," I say, moving closer to him. "As long as they don't involve changing the fundamental structure of our relationship every three days."

He laughs, pulling me into his arms. "I think I can manage that."

Chapter 10

Grand Gestures and a Ring Box

Nate

Four months after the Peterson project launched, I'm sitting in my office reviewing quarterly reports when Jake Williams knocks on my door frame.

"Got a minute, Nate? I wanted to update you on the Peterson situation."

"Please tell me Mrs. Peterson didn't decide she wants to relocate the entire kitchen to the second floor," I say, looking up from my computer.

Jake grins. "Actually, quite the opposite. She loved Courtney's alternative design solutions so much that she's referring us to three of her friends. Apparently word is getting around about how well we handled her… creative requests."

"Seriously?"

"Seriously. Courtney turned our most difficult client into our biggest advocate." Jake settles into the chair across from my desk. "I've never seen anyone handle client relations the way she does. She's got this ability to make people feel heard while still keeping them grounded in reality."

Pride swells in my chest. "She's pretty amazing."

"She is. And speaking of amazing project managers, I heard through the grapevine that she's being considered for a promotion?"

"Where did you hear that?"

"Brett may have mentioned something about creating a senior director position. Something about recognizing exceptional talent when he sees it."

After Jake leaves, I find myself staring out my office window, thinking about how much has changed in the past several months. The Peterson project success is the latest in a string of wins for Courtney. She's handled every challenge thrown her way with grace, creativity, and the professional excellence that makes everyone around her better at their jobs.

My phone buzzes with a text from Courtney:

Peterson final walkthrough at 3. Want to come see your girlfriend's masterpiece?

Wouldn't miss it. Your boyfriend is very proud of you.

Courtney: Good, because I have surprise plans for dinner tonight. Dress nice.

THE PETERSON HOUSE LOOKS INCREDIBLE. What started as a nightmare project has transformed into something that belongs in a home design magazine. Every detail reflects Courtney's ability to listen to her clients' dreams while steering them toward practical, beautiful solutions.

"Mrs. Peterson, the kitchen turned out beautifully," I tell our client as we complete the final walkthrough.

"Oh, it's perfect! Absolutely perfect!" Mrs. Peterson beams, running her hands along the marble countertops. "Courtney, you are a miracle worker. I can't believe you took my crazy Pinterest idea and turned it into something even better."

"That's what we're here for," Courtney says with a smile. "To help you create the home of your dreams."

"Well, you certainly did that. And I've already given your information to Linda Blake and the Reynolds. They're both planning renovations next year. Plus, Mr. Peterson is talking with Brett about his commercial properties too."

As we drive back to the office, I can't stop stealing glances at Courtney. She's practically glowing with satisfaction and seeing her this happy and confident makes my chest tight with affection.

"So," I say as we pull into the Hearthstone Homes

parking lot, "what's this surprise dinner you've got planned?"

"You'll see. Pick me up at seven, and don't ask any more questions."

"Bossy."

"You love it when I'm bossy."

"I love everything about you," I tell her, and the simple truth of it still catches me off guard sometimes.

At exactly seven p.m., I'm standing on Courtney's doorstep in my best suit, wondering what she has planned. When she opens the door, my breath catches. She's wearing a red dress that hugs her curves perfectly and makes her look like she's stepped out of a dream.

"Wow," I breathe. "You look incredible."

"Thank you." She grabs a small clutch and a wrap. "Ready for your surprise?"

"More than ready."

She directs me to drive to the historic downtown area, and I'm surprised when she tells me to park outside Magnolia Moon.

"This is where we had our first date," I point out.

"Exactly." Her smile is mysterious as she takes my arm. "I thought it was time we made this officially our place."

But instead of going inside the restaurant, she leads me around the building to the outdoor patio area. And that's when I see it—the entire space has been transformed. Twinkling lights are strung everywhere, creating a canopy of stars above a single table set for two.

Candles flicker in glass hurricanes, rose petals are scattered across the table, and soft music plays from hidden speakers.

"Courtney," I breathe, taking in the romantic scene. "What is this?"

"This is me planning a grand gesture for you," she says, her voice slightly nervous. "You gave me the mountain getaway, you planned our perfect first date, you've been so patient while I figured out my professional insecurities. I wanted to do something special for you."

"You did all this?"

"I had help. Mrs. Havers knows people, and Lia has excellent taste in romantic lighting." She takes my hands, looking up at me with those beautiful blue eyes. "Nate, these past four months have been the best of my life. Not just because of the romance, but because of the partnership. The way we work together, support each other, challenge each other to be better."

"Courtney—"

"Let me finish," she says, and there's something in her voice that makes me pay attention. "I've spent my whole life trying to prove that I deserve good things, that I've earned my place, that I'm worthy of love and success and happiness. But with you, I don't have to prove anything. You see me—really see me—and love me, anyway."

"I love you because of who you are, not despite it," I tell her. "You get that, right?"

"I'm starting to." She takes a deep breath, gathering courage for something. "Nate, we've only been officially together for four months, and some people would say this is too fast, but I know what I want."

"What do you want?"

"I want forever with you. I want to build a life together, create new traditions, support each other through whatever comes next." She pauses, and her next words come out in a rush. "I want to marry you, Nate Brockington."

My heart stops. "Courtney—"

"I'm not proposing," she says quickly, her cheeks flushing pink. "I'm... I'm putting it out there. That this is what I want, when you're ready. If you're ready. Whenever you're ready."

I stare at her for a moment, this incredible woman who laid her heart on the line in the most beautiful way possible. Then I start laughing, which makes her face fall.

"Why are you laughing?" she asks, looking hurt and confused.

"Because," I say, reaching into my jacket pocket and pulling out the small velvet box I've been carrying around for three weeks, "I was going to propose to you."

Her eyes go wide as she takes in the ring box. "You were?"

"I was. I had this whole speech planned about how you've changed my life, how you make me want to be the best version of myself, how I can't imagine a future that doesn't include you." I drop to one knee right there on the patio, surrounded by rose petals. "But since you beat me to the romantic gesture..."

"Nate," she whispers, her hands flying to her mouth.

"Courtney Hartwell," I say, opening the ring box to reveal the solitaire oval diamond ring I picked out with Beth's help, "will you marry me? Will you let me spend the rest of my life making you as happy as you've made me?"

"Yes," she says, tears streaming down her face. "Yes, yes, obviously yes."

I slide the ring onto her finger, and it fits perfectly—like everything else about us. When I stand up, she launches herself into my arms, kissing me like her life depends on it.

"I can't believe you were going to propose too," she says against my lips.

"Great minds think alike," I tell her, spinning her around as the reality of it sinks in. "We're engaged."

"We're engaged," she agrees, laughing and crying at the same time. "Oh my god, Mrs. Havers is going to be so smug about this."

"She's going to plan our entire wedding before we even set a date."

"Let her. I'm too happy to care about anything except the fact that I get to marry my best friend."

As we sit down to the romantic dinner she arranged, I think about the journey that brought us here. From colleagues to friends to lovers to partners, and now to fiancé. It hasn't always been easy—we've had to navigate personal insecurities, and the challenge of building something real in the midst of very public scrutiny.

But looking at Courtney across the candlelit table, wearing my ring and smiling like she's never been happier, I know we've built something strong enough to last a lifetime.

"So," she says, cutting into her salmon, "when do you want to get married?"

"Tomorrow?" I suggest, only half joking.

"Tempting." She considers this seriously. "What about a Christmas wedding? Something romantic and festive, with snow and twinkling lights and all the fairy tale elements?"

"Perfect," I agree, though honestly, I'd marry her in a courthouse tomorrow if that's what she wanted. "As long as it's you walking down the aisle toward me, I don't care about anything else."

"It will be," she promises, reaching across the table to take my hand. "For the rest of our lives, it's going to be me walking toward you and you walking toward me. Partners in everything."

"Partners in everything," I agree, bringing her hand to my lips to kiss the ring I placed there.

Later that night, as we're curled up together on her couch, Courtney traces patterns on my chest and sighs contentedly.

"Guess what I realized tonight?" she says.

"What?"

"Remember when we were planning your bachelor auction date, and you asked me what would make me happy?"

"I remember."

"From the moment Mrs. Havers told me you were going to be in the bachelor auction, I knew I couldn't let anyone else have you."

"Good thing, because I was only ever going to be yours anyway."

She lifts her head to look at me, and in her eyes I glimpse our entire future—the house we'll build together, the traditions we'll create, the family we might have someday, the partnership that will sustain us through whatever comes next.

"I love you, Nate Brockington."

"I love you too, future Mrs. Brockington."

"Oh, I like the sound of that," she says with a grin. "Mrs. Courtney Brockington. Courtney Hartwell-Brockington. What do you think?"

"I think," I say, pulling her up for a kiss, "that you can call yourself whatever makes you happy, as long as you call yourself mine."

"Always," she promises against my lips.

Epilogue: Cabin Fever and Mountain Surprises

Nate

I pull into the parking lot of Blue Ridge Mountain Resort and sense that familiar surge of anticipation I've come to associate with any time alone with Courtney. The resort is where I'd hoped to bring her months ago, when I gifted her this romantic getaway at the Valentine's charity event and praying she'd want my company. Now here we are, engaged for two months, wedding planned for Christmas, and this weekend is like the perfect chance to slow down and breathe, catch the autumn colors, before the holiday chaos begins.

Courtney stretches in the passenger seat as I turn off the engine. She looks beautiful in her hiking clothes—practical but somehow still managing to make athletic wear look elegant.

"Worth the wait?" I ask, grabbing our bags from the back.

"Ask me again after our couples massage tomorrow."

Her grin is infectious as she takes in the rustic stone buildings nestled against the mountainside. "Though I have to say, this place is even more gorgeous than the brochures made it look."

The check-in process is smooth, and soon we're being led to our cabin—the same type I'd imagined us staying in all those months ago, complete with a stone fireplace, wall of windows overlooking the lake, and that king-size bed with the rustic log headboard.

"This is perfect," Courtney breathes, moving to the windows to take in the view. "I can see why you thought I'd love it here. Fall is my favorite time of year; the colors are amazing."

I set our bags down and move behind her, wrapping my arms around her waist. "I was hoping we'd get to use those hiking trails tomorrow. Maybe pack a lunch, spend the day exploring."

"Sounds amazing." She leans back against me, and I can sense some of the tension she's been carrying leave her shoulders. "I need this. Work has been insane with the new Blake project, and wedding planning is—"

She stops mid-sentence, her body going rigid in my arms.

"You okay?"

"I..." She presses a hand to her mouth, her face suddenly pale. "I think I need to—"

She doesn't finish the sentence before she's racing to the bathroom. I hear her retching, and my chest tightens with concern. She's been working too hard lately, barely eating, stressed about the wedding details.

When she emerges a few minutes later, she appears shaky and embarrassed.

"Sorry," she says, sinking onto the edge of the bed. "I think I might be coming down with something. Maybe I picked up a bug somewhere."

"Don't apologize." I sit beside her, pressing the back of my hand to her forehead. "You're not feverish. When did this start?"

"Three days, maybe? I felt a little queasy when I woke up, but I thought it was just wedding stress." She attempts a smile. "So much for our romantic hiking adventure."

"Hey." I take her hands in mine. "We have the whole weekend. Rest is more important than hiking."

Over the next hour, I watch her try to keep down crackers and ginger ale, but everything comes back up. She doesn't have a fever, but she's getting weaker, and I'm starting to worry.

"I'm calling Lia," I announce, pulling out my phone.

"Nate, you don't need to—"

"Yes, I do." I'm already scrolling to her contact. "You can't keep anything down, and I want to make sure we're not missing something."

Lia picks up on the second ring. "Hey, how's the romantic mountain getaway?"

"Not so romantic at the moment. Courtney's been

throwing up for the past couple hours. No fever, but she can't keep anything down. Should I be worried?"

"Hmm. Could be a stomach bug, could be food poisoning. Has she eaten anything unusual lately?"

"Not that I know of. Same stuff we always eat."

"Any other symptoms? Headache, body aches, fatigue?"

I look over at Courtney, who's curled up on the bed looking miserable. "Fatigue, definitely. But that could be from being sick. She said started about three days ago?"

"When was her last period?"

The question catches me off guard. "I… I don't know. Why?"

"Hand me the phone, Nate," Courtney says quietly from the bed.

I pass her the phone, and I can only hear her side of the conversation.

"Hey, Lia… Yeah, I feel awful… No fever… August? God, maybe late August?… What?… Are you serious?… Oh my god…"

I watch the color drain completely from Courtney's face. She sits up straighter, one hand going to her stomach.

"I didn't even think… We've been so busy with wedding planning and work… Okay… Yes, I'll get one… Thanks, Lia."

She hands the phone back to me, and I can hear Lia's voice on the other end.

"Nate? I'm sending in a prescription for anti-nausea

medication to the pharmacy in town. But I also think Courtney should pick up a pregnancy test while she's there."

My heart stops. "A what?"

"It's probably nothing, but the timing and symptoms... it's worth ruling out. Call me after you take a test, okay?"

"Okay," I manage, though my voice sounds strange to my own ears.

After I hang up, Courtney and I stare at each other in silence for a long moment.

"A pregnancy test," she says finally.

"A pregnancy test," I repeat.

"I mean, we've been careful. Mostly careful. But there was that night last month when we got carried away and—"

"The night after the Morrison project celebration," I finish.

"Yeah." She takes a shaky breath. "God, Nate, what if—"

"Hey." I move to sit beside her on the bed. "Whatever it is, we'll handle it together, okay? But first, let's go get that medication so you feel better."

The drive into town is quiet, both of us lost in our own thoughts. The local pharmacy is small but well-stocked, and the pharmacist is friendly and discreet. Courtney picks up the anti-nausea prescription and, after a moment of hesitation, adds a pregnancy test to the counter.

Back at the cabin, she takes the anti-nausea medication first, and within thirty minutes, the constant nausea eases.

"Better?" I ask.

"Much." She's got some color back in her cheeks. "Okay. I guess… I guess I should take the test."

"Do you want me to wait outside?"

"No. Stay with me."

I follow her into the bathroom, and she reads the instructions on the box twice before opening it.

"Three minutes," she says, setting the test on the counter. "We wait three minutes."

Those three minutes are like three hours. We sit on the bathroom floor, backs against the tub, and I hold her hand while we wait.

"What are you thinking?" I ask.

"I'm thinking this is insane timing. We're getting married in two months. This wasn't in the plan."

"But?"

She looks at me, with a mix of fear and something else in her eyes. "But I'm also thinking that if it's positive, I'm not sorry."

My chest tightens with an emotion I can't quite name. "Me neither."

The timer on her phone goes off, and we both freeze.

"You look," she says. "I can't."

I stand up and move to the counter, looking down at the little plastic window. Two pink lines. Clear as day.

"Courtney," I say softly.

"What does it say?"

I turn to face her, and I can't keep the smile off my face. "It says we're having a baby."

Her hand flies to her mouth, tears immediately filling her eyes. "Really?"

"Really." I kneel beside her, taking her hands in mine. "We're having a baby."

"Oh my god." She starts laughing and crying at the same time. "We're having a baby. Nate, we're having a baby."

"How do you feel about that?" I ask, studying her face.

"Terrified," she admits. "But also... incredibly happy. Is that crazy?"

"If it's crazy, then I'm crazy too." I pull her into my arms, holding her close. "I love you. I love our baby. I love that we get to do this together."

"The timing is insane," she says against my chest. "Christmas wedding, and I might be showing by then."

"So who cares, I'll have the most beautiful pregnant bride in Georgia."

"What if I'm sick during the ceremony?"

"Then we'll have a bucket ready behind the altar."

She laughs, pulling back to look at me. "You're okay with this? We never talked about kids."

"Courtney, I've been ready for forever with you since the night you bid on me at that auction. A baby only makes forever start a little sooner than we planned." I rest my hand on her still-flat stomach. "Besides, this little one was conceived in love. How can that be anything but perfect?"

"When you put it like that..." She covers my hand with hers. "I love you, Nate Brockington. You and this baby."

"I love you too, future Mrs. Brockington. Both of you."

As the sun sets over the mountains outside our cabin window, we lie in bed talking about everything—names and nurseries and how we're going to tell our families. The hiking can wait for another trip. Right now, all I want is to hold my fiancée and think about the life we're building together.

"You know what this means, don't you?" Courtney says, curled up against my side.

"What?"

"Mrs. Havers is going to take credit for this too. The charity auction that led to our relationship, and now a Christmas baby to go with our Christmas wedding."

I laugh, pressing a kiss to the top of her head. "She's going to be insufferable."

"She's going to be the best honorary grandmother this baby could ask for."

"True." I tighten my arms around her. "Think she'll let us name it ourselves, or will she have opinions about that too?"

"Oh, she'll have opinions. Probably a whole list of suggestions organized by gender and middle name compatibility."

Outside, the mountain air is crisp and clear, the yellow and red leaves abundant with autumn fills with the promise of new beginnings. In a few months, we'll be married. In a few more months after that, we'll be parents. It's not the timeline we planned, but it's ours.

And I can't wait for what comes next.

"Hey, Nate?"

"Yeah?"

"I love you."

Courtney tilts her head up to look at me, and in her eyes, I witness our entire future—the wedding, the baby, the life we're building together one surprising moment at a time. I'm so fulfilled and in love it's a happiness, I never thought I'd experience. This woman is my life.

"I love you more." I respond.

Then she's kissing me, and I'm kissing her back, and somewhere in the distance I can hear the sound of our happily-ever-after beginning.

The End

Author's Note

Did you enjoy **Cupid's Sweet Conspiracy?** 💕

If Courtney and Nate's story made you swoon, smile, or sigh in the best way—please consider leaving a review. Just a few words from *you* helps other readers discover the magic of Peachwood Grove—and it means the world to me as an author.

Thank you for reading, and for spreading the bookish cheer!

Did you love Courtney and Nate?
Want more - check out their bonus scene:
https://ckdarling.com/bonus-fun

Can't get enough of Peachwood Grove's matchmaking mischief?

You'll love ***Snowed in at Spruce Ridge*** — where Mrs. Havers works her holiday magic on two feuding Christmas tree farmers who definitely weren't planning to fall in love.

Rivals-to-lovers. One snowstorm. One cozy fireplace.

Short, spicy, and oh-so-swoon-worthy. A one-hour read! Keep the holiday sparks flying!

GRAB Your FREE Book

Also by C.K. Darling

This is the third book in **The Holiday Matchmaker Series**. The last story in this series is coming later in 2026.

And coming in the summer of 2026, **The Blazing Hearts Series**. Get ready for the McCallister brothers—three firefighters who fight flames by day and set hearts ablaze by night.

Embers of Fate, Book 1

A Fated Romance between Ryan and Ember

More in Peachwood Grove...

The Blazing Heart Series (Summer 2026)

Book 1 - Embers of Fate

Book 2 - Ashes and Sparks

Book 3 - Fiery Attractions

Sweetheart Scones & Stories Series

The Holiday Matchmaker Series

Acknowledgments

To my darling readers—thank y'all for once again returning to Peachwood Grove, where love has a habit of showing up right when it's meant to. Courtney and Nate's story is one of quiet longing, brave vulnerability, and finally stepping into the love that's been there all along. Thank you for cheering for them, for swooning with me, and for believing—just as I do—that romance deserves to be joyful, heartfelt, and a little spicier.

To my wonderful editor, **Aime at Red Leaf Words**—thank you for your heart, clarity, and brilliance. You don't just refine my stories; you've helped me grow into a stronger, braver, better storyteller. I am deeply grateful for you and your steady wisdom.

To **Angela Haas**—thank you for being my creative chaos partner, cheerleader, voice-note sounding board, and cherished friend. I adore you.

To **High Gravity Productions**—thank you for making Peachwood Grove sound like pure romance magic. And to **Andi Eloise** and **Ryan Lee Dunlap**—oh my goodness… emotions incoming. This book marks the final chapter of your journey in this world with me, and goodness… talk about the end of an era. Seven books, countless swoons, unforgettable chemistry, and so much magic. You've breathed soul, humor, heat, and heart into these stories, and I couldn't be more grateful. Thank you for loving these characters as deeply as I do.

To my husband, **Butch**—thank you for the laughter, the romance, and the steady love that grounds me. You are my favorite forever.

With all my Southern gratitude and a sprinkle of Valentine sweetness—thank you for reading, listening, reviewing, and sharing these stories. May love surprise you, delight you, and always feel worth the risk.

About the Author

C.K. Darling crafts witty, spicy contemporary romances set in the charming town of Peachwood Grove, Georgia. Specializing in quick reads for busy romance readers. C.K.'s stories deliver all the emotion and satisfaction in under two hours. Away from her desk, C.K. is either concocting the next heartwarming tale in Peachwood Grove, dabbling in arts and crafts, or enjoying the charms of Southern life with her family and beloved pets.

facebook.com/ckdarlingauthor
threads.com/@ckdarlingauthor
instagram.com/ckdarlingauthor
tiktok.com/@ckdarlingauthor
bookbub.com/authors/c-k-darling

* 9 7 8 1 9 5 6 0 4 9 3 0 5 *
BVPRI - #0012 - 280126 - C0 - 198/129/8 - PB - 9781956049305 - Gloss Lamination